Cricket's New Friend

After breakfast, Cricket and her father took Buster out to the backyard. He turned out to be a champion Frisbee player, leaping and catching the Frisbee almost every time it was thrown.

"You're some dog, Buster," Cricket's father laughed. "But I'm afraid you've worn me out."

"Me, too," said Cricket, trying to dodge the slobbery Frisbee that Buster kept shoving at her. How could Buster's owner have kept up with him? she wondered. And where was she now?

Cricket dropped down on the lawn where Buster was lying, panting in the cool grass. Maybe Buster's owner would never show up, she thought. Maybe she and Buster could lie here forever.

Then, just as she'd closed her eyes and was imagining the two of them playing in a Frisbee tournament, the doorbell rang.

Cricket Goes to the Dogs

Susan Meyers

little rainbow ®

Troll Associates

For Cricket Bird, with thanks for her friendship and her name.

Chapter

Cricket Connors had never wanted anything so much in all her life. "Oh, they are so darling!" she exclaimed, kneeling down beside the big wooden box full of squirming golden brown puppies. The pups' mother, a magnificent golden retriever, looked up at her hopefully and thumped her tail. "I can hardly believe it. Last week there were none and now there are ten. It's like a miracle, isn't it?"

Mrs. Wilson, the owner of the Sunny Hill Kennels, smiled. Cricket, who was ten years old and in the fifth grade at Redwood Grove Elementary School, had been visiting the kennel nearly every day for the past week, waiting for the puppies to be born. Mrs. Wilson looked forward to seeing her eager face, dotted with freckles and framed by curly red hair, peering expectantly into the whelping room where the puppies were due to be born. And she was always interested to see what

Cricket was wearing. Today it was zebra-striped tights, a yellow polka-dotted shirt, and an Indian vest embroidered with yellow and red flowers.

Cricket had told Mrs. Wilson all about herself: how she'd had a golden retriever named Pete ("the best dog in the world") who'd died just last year, how she wanted to be a veterinarian or a zookeeper when she grew up, how she had an old friend named Jenny who'd moved away and a new friend named Meg Kelly who'd just arrived in Redwood Grove, and how she and Meg and some other girls were starting a club.

But most of all Cricket and Mrs. Wilson had talked about dogs, about how absolutely wonderful they were, and about how everyone—especially a ten-year-old girl who wanted to be a vet when she grew up—needed to have one of her own.

"I know what you mean," said the kennel owner now, kneeling down beside Cricket as the day-old pups, their eyes tightly shut, scrambled over each other, trying to find the best place to nurse. "No matter how many litters I raise, I always get excited about new puppies. Would you like to hold one?"

Those were exactly the words Cricket had been hoping to hear!

"Go ahead," Mrs. Wilson urged. "Cindy won't mind. She's an old hand at this motherhood business." She scratched the pups' mother behind the ears to reassure her, as Cricket—who didn't need to be asked twice—reached into the box and scooped up a golden

8

brown puppy.

"Oh, it's so sweet!" she murmured, cradling the puppy's warm little body in her hands. It snuffled blindly against her fingers as if trying to figure out where it was. She stroked its velvety ears, folded into tiny triangles at the sides of its head, and rubbed her cheek against its silky, sweet-smelling fur. There was no doubt about it. Cricket was in love. She *had* to have one of these puppies. "How long before they can leave their mother?" she asked.

"Two months. Maybe a bit more," Mrs. Wilson replied. "I'm very careful about my pups. I like to be sure they've had a good start in life before they go to new homes. To tell you the truth, sometimes I hate to part with them."

Cricket could certainly understand that. If she had a dog like Cindy and a litter of ten beautiful puppies, she wouldn't part with a single one of them! "You will sell them though, won't you?" she asked, suddenly anxious. What if Mrs. Wilson really wasn't able to give them up? "Is the price still two hundred dollars?"

"Afraid so," the kennel owner replied. "I know it's a lot, but what with food and shots and vet's bills, they're expensive to raise. I already have deposits on three of them. Cindy's puppies always go fast, so if you're serious about getting one, you'd better have your parents call me soon so we can make arrangements. I usually ask for a deposit of one hundred dollars now and the rest when the pup's ready to leave, but if that's too much, maybe we can work something out. I know how much you want one."

"Oh, but it isn't," said Cricket. "*I'm* the one who's paying for the puppy and I've already got one hundred dollars. That is, I will have one hundred dollars as soon as I—Oh my gosh!" she interrupted herself. "What time is it?"

Mrs. Wilson checked her watch. "Quarter to eleven."

"Oh, no, I'm going to be late for our very first meeting! And that's where I'm getting the money. At least, I *hope* I'm getting the money." Cricket gave the puppy she was holding a quick kiss on the nose and returned it to its mother. "Don't worry. I'll explain later," she said, seeing the puzzled expression on the kennel owner's face. "No time now. Got to go!"

Cricket dashed out the door to the driveway where her bike was parked. A big pink cake box filled with tarts that her mother, who ran a catering business, had made for the meeting was in the basket attached to the handlebars. Swinging her leg over the seat, Cricket pushed off and coasted down the drive into the bike lane that bordered the street.

The meeting was being held in Meg Kelly's grandparents' house, where Meg, her little brother Kevin, and her mother were living until they could find a place of their own. The house was on the opposite side of town from the kennel. It would take at least fifteen minutes, pedaling fast, to get there. But they wouldn't start without her. They couldn't. After all, if it hadn't been for her—and Meg, too, of course—there wouldn't even be an Always Friends Club!

Always Friends. Cricket whizzed around a corner, her yellow shirt billowing in the breeze, and thought about the club that was going to bring her the money—that she *hoped* was going to bring her the money—to buy one of Cindy's adorable puppies. It was an amazing story. Even now Cricket could hardly believe it. It had all started with the discovery of an old scrapbook buried at the bottom of a footlocker in the attic of Meg Kelly's grandparents' house.

Cricket had met Meg, who'd just moved to Redwood Grove from Los Angeles, at school and she'd liked her right from the start. She'd liked Meg's long blonde hair and her friendly eyes, and the brightly flowered dress she'd been wearing (which in Cricket's opinion was a lot more interesting than the boring old sweaters and jeans that most kids at Redwood Grove Elementary wore). When she found out that both of them had had best friends named Jenny (Meg's was still in Los Angeles and Cricket's had moved to Alaska), she was sure they were meant to be friends.

What's more, she'd had a feeling there was some sort of mysterious connection between them—as if they'd known each other for a long, long time, maybe even in another life. Cricket often had feelings like that. Her friends—especially Amy—were always teasing her about it. But this time she'd been right!

She shivered even now just thinking about it, remembering that afternoon in the attic and how Meg had pulled the scrapbook from the bottom of the foot-locker filled with her mother's childhood treasures, how she'd opened the cover (in spite of the word *SECRET!* printed on it), and how they'd discovered from the photographs pasted inside that their mothers, who'd both grown up in Redwood Grove, had been childhood best friends!

It was hard to say who'd been more excited—Cricket and Meg, who felt like they were practically sisters, or their mothers, who'd lost track of each other over the years, and were overjoyed to be together again. As for the club . . . well, that's what the scrapbook was all about. The big red-covered album was chock full of photos and souvenirs from a club their mothers had started when they were girls.

The name of the club was Always Friends. The five club members had carried out all kinds of money-making projects—everything from putting on backyard circuses to making doll clothes and weeding gardens. Instead of dividing up the money they earned from each project, they put it together and chose one girl—by pulling her name out of a hat—to spend it. That way each girl got a chance to have more than she ever could have earned on her own.

It was a terrific idea. So terrific that Cricket and Meg had immediately decided to start an Always Friends Club of their own. They'd recruited Cricket's friend Amy Chan and a new girl named Brittany Logan to be members. And before they'd even had a chance to hold a meeting, they managed to earn $25 each— $100 in all—by taking part in a focus group at the computer software company where Meg's mother worked. That had been last Saturday, when Cindy was still bulging with unborn puppies and the idea of getting one was just a glimmer in Cricket's mind. Now, with $25 in her shirt pocket, and $75 more in the other girls' hands, she actually had a chance.

Steadying the cake box in her bike basket, she turned onto Cascade Drive, where Meg's grandparents lived. The big brown-shingled house was at the end of the block. She could see its stone chimney and peaked roof above the branches of the trees. From beneath the eaves, a small round window peered out over the street like a watchful eye. Behind that window was the attic—the secret attic—where she and Meg had found the scrapbook. They were going to hold their first meeting there. They were going to pick the name of the girl who got to spend the club money out of an old straw hat they'd found hanging from a pair of deer antlers nailed to the attic wall.

It's *has* to be me, Cricket thought, gripping her handlebars tightly. She knew she shouldn't count on it. Her head told her not to. But deep down in her heart she was sure she'd be chosen. After all, hadn't she seen the first star in the sky yesterday evening and made a wish on it? And hadn't she had a dream just last night about a dog coming to live in her house? True, it hadn't been a sweet little golden-colored puppy. It had been a big, shaggy white dog with dirty fur and muddy feet. Still . . . it had to mean something, didn't it? Her heart beat faster at the thought of it and she put on an extra burst of speed, covering the rest of the block in nothing flat.

Meg spotted her the moment she pulled into the drive. "Where have you been?" she yelled, leaning out of her bedroom window on the second floor of the house. "We thought you'd never get here."

Amy Chan joined her. "You'd better have the food," she shouted, poking her head out the window beside Meg. Her shiny black ponytails glistened in the sun. "Otherwise we're not going to let you come in!"

"Don't pay any attention to them." Meg's mother and little brother, Kevin, came out onto the front porch as Cricket parked her bike, grabbed the cake box from the basket, and hurried up the walk to the house. "They've already gone through two bags of pretzels."

"Where's Brittany?" Kevin demanded, staring at Cricket suspiciously as she climbed up the porch steps. "I don't want her. I want Brittany!" His four-year-old face, round and pink-cheeked under a mop of curly blond hair, clouded over.

"Oh, dear, he's got the most enormous crush on that girl," Mrs. Kelly said, taking the cake box from Cricket's hands and herding her and Kevin into the spacious front hall of the house. Colorful throw rugs

14

were scattered about and a wide staircase led up to the second floor. "Ever since that sleepover last week when Brittany let him hold her hand during the *Jungle Book* video, he's been smitten. Don't take it personally," she added. "I'm sure he likes you, too. Mmm, these smell good." She sniffed the cake box. "Karen—I mean, your mother—called to say they need to be heated in a 350-degree oven. They're some new kind of cheese tarts she made for a wedding this afternoon. Have you tasted them?"

"I didn't have time," said Cricket. "I don't think Dad tried them either. He's been busy patching up the roof on our house because the last time it rained we had leaks everywhere. I hope they're okay," she added anxiously. "Mom's been making some pretty weird-tasting stuff lately. I don't know why. Usually everything she cooks is delicious."

"You can say that again!" exclaimed Meg, appearing at the top of the staircase. She was a big fan of Mrs. Connors's cooking. "But don't. We've got to start this meeting."

"But you can't start without Brittany!" Kevin protested. "You said she was coming. I want to see Brittany."

Meg rolled her eyes. "I said she was *not* coming, Kevin. Don't you ever listen?"

Kevin's lip began to tremble.

"Now, Kevin," Mrs. Kelly said quickly, taking him by the hand. "We've had enough of that. We'll just put these snacks in the oven and then maybe Grandpa will take you to the park."

"But I want to see Brittany!"

"Aren't you glad you're an only child," said Meg to Cricket as Kevin began to wail. "Better get up here quick before he decides to take it out on you."

Cricket was sure she was kidding. Kevin was really a sweet little boy, no matter how he was acting right now. Still, she didn't waste any time dashing up the stairs. She reached the second-floor hall just as Amy came out of Meg's room.

Amy was a sturdy, sensible-looking girl who spent most of her time in sweatpants and a Redwood Grove Junior Soccer League sweatshirt, which was what she was wearing right now. She had three older brothers, so she knew what she was talking about when she said, "They only get worse. All my brothers think about these days is girls. Lucky *they* haven't met Brittany!"

"But where is she?" Cricket asked, keeping her voice down so Kevin, who was being dragged down the hall by his mother, wouldn't hear. "Is she really not coming?"

"She has a riding lesson," Meg said.

"A riding lesson?" Cricket felt a sudden sharp pang of envy. Riding lessons were exactly what she'd always wanted to take. She could just picture herself galloping over fields and streams, leaping fences astride a magnificent steed—a black stallion maybe, like the one in her favorite book. But horses and riding lessons were expensive. Her father, who was a high school teacher, and her mother, who had a business that was barely breaking even, couldn't afford things like that.

For Brittany, of course, it was different. Brittany Logan, besides being beautiful and looking like she'd just stepped out of the pages of a fashion magazine, had lived in Paris and New York and gone to an exclusive Swiss boarding school before moving to Redwood Grove a few weeks ago. She spoke French as well as English and had a mother who was a famous fashion designer and a father who traveled around on business trips in limousines and private jets.

It went without saying that she was rich. Her parents could probably buy Cindy's whole litter of puppies if they wanted, Cricket thought, feeling another sharp jab of envy. She forgot that Brittany had told Meg, who'd recruited her for the club, that she got only a small allowance to spend and had to do her share of household chores, too. She was every bit as eager as the rest of them to earn money of her own.

"Well, I think it's pretty selfish of her," Cricket said now. "She knew we were holding a meeting. Couldn't she have gone riding some other time?"

"Apparently not," said Meg, leading the way into her room as Kevin's shouts faded in the background. "This is her first lesson with some fancy new teacher. Her mother set it up without telling her. She felt really bad when she called to tell me this morning. You know how she worries about things."

"I'll say," said Amy. "I've never known anyone who worries so much. She's always afraid she'll do the wrong thing."

"That's because she's led such a weird life. She's moved around a lot and she hasn't had a chance to get to know many kids her own age," said Meg, who felt responsible for Brittany and worried about how she was going to fit into the club. "The important thing is she said we should go on with the meeting without her. She doesn't want us to wait. She even said we could put her name in the hat."

"She did? Well, that's different," said Cricket. "I was afraid we weren't going to be able to have the meeting. I thought we might not be able to pick my name out of—I mean . . ." She blushed as Amy and Meg looked at her suspiciously. "I mean, come on. Let's go up to the attic. The first meeting of the Always Friends Club is about to come to order!"

C h a p t e r

A trapdoor hidden in the ceiling of Meg's closet was the only way into the attic. Meg hadn't known it was there until she and Cricket found it last week, and Amy hadn't had a chance to see it until today.

"This is amazing," she said, as Meg took a flashlight from her night table, led the way into the closet, and shone the light up at the ceiling to reveal the outline of the trapdoor cut into the boards. At one end was a set of hinges, at the other a metal ring. "How did you two ever find it?"

"Cricket gets credit for that," Meg said. "She's the one who figured it out."

"Well, it wasn't too hard," Cricket admitted modestly. "I had a friend in first grade whose family lived in one of these big old houses in the redwoods, and I remembered how they got into their attic. All you have to do is pull on that metal ring. The door opens and a stairway—a sort of slanting ladder—comes down."

"It's like that story where the kids step into an old wardrobe and find a whole new world, isn't it?" Amy said. "What's that book called?"

"*The Lion, the Witch, and the Wardrobe*. One of my favorites," replied Meg, who was a big reader. She wanted to be a writer when she grew up and she'd already thought about how neat it would be to write a story about a house with a secret attic. "There aren't any lions or witches up here, though," she added. "Just lots and lots of spiders, judging from all the webs my grandfather and I found when we cleaned yesterday. Now stand back." She took a bent clothes hanger from a corner of the closet and hooked it into the metal ring. "This door comes down fast. It can hit you on the head if you're not careful. That's why my grandparents kept the attic secret until now. They didn't want me going up when I was just a little kid. Ready?"

Cricket and Amy stepped back. Meg gave the ring a sharp jerk, and the trapdoor swung open. A slanted stairway slid down—just as Cricket had said it would—hitting the floor with a thud.

"Wow!" exclaimed Amy, as light from the attic flooded into the closet.

"Go on up," Meg urged.

Amy didn't need any encouragement. By the time Meg spoke she was already halfway up the stairway. "This is terrific! A perfect place for a meeting," she called down. "Brittany doesn't know what she's missing."

Cricket climbed up next. She was already thinking about what she'd do when her name was picked from the hat. She'd run downstairs and phone Mrs. Wilson. Then she'd jump on her bike and race straight to the kennel. She could practically feel the puppy's warm little body in her hands. Of course she wouldn't be able to bring it home yet, but that didn't matter. She could visit it every day. She could—

But the sight of the attic as she climbed through the trapdoor made her stop thinking about Cindy's puppies. "Wow!" she said, echoing Amy. Her eyes opened wide in astonishment. "You and your grandfather must have really worked hard, Meg. This place was a mess when we found it last week."

"More than a mess," said Meg, climbing up the stairway after her. "It took us all yesterday afternoon to clean it up. We swept and dusted and even washed the windows. See how much brighter it is."

She was right. The attic, which had been bathed in a ghostly yellowish glow when Cricket and Meg found it last week, was now bright with sunlight that streamed in through the sparkling clean windows under the eaves. In addition, Meg and her grandfather had shoved all the boxes and trunks, piles of old magazines, and other stuff aside to clear a space in the middle of the floor. They'd rolled out a threadbare Turkish carpet and made a sort of sofa out of an old lounge chair cushion and a pile of pillows. The footlocker where the scrapbook had been hidden was set up as a table. On top of it was the scrapbook itself.

"Oh, I've been dying to see this," said Amy, picking up the big, red-covered album. "I want to find out exactly what this club did, so I'll know what we're in for." She opened the cover. "Hey, look at this. The minutes of their first meeting—September 1968. That was practically the dark ages! I bet they didn't even have television!"

She plopped herself down on the lounge chair cushion and began eagerly turning the pages. "It looks like they put on a terrific backyard circus, though. And made doll clothes. And gave pony rides. And put out a newspaper."

Cricket, who'd already seen all the photographs and souvenirs in the album, turned to something else perched on top of the footlocker—a stuffed owl! "Where in the world did you get that?" she asked, staring at the moth-eaten bird. It stared back at her through its yellow glass eyes.

"You mean the owl? Isn't it great!" said Meg. "Mom found it when she was rummaging around up here. She said it used to sit on the mantelpiece in the den where they held their meetings. Grandma refused to put it down there again, so I thought we could keep it up here. Sort of like a mascot. And my grandfather found this gavel for us." She picked up a wooden hammer lying at the owl's feet. "You use it to call a meeting to order."

Amy's ears perked up at the sound of that. "Well, what are we waiting for?" she said. "Brittany's not coming, but the rest of us are here. Let's do it!"

Meg shot a quick glance at Cricket. She was suddenly struck by what an amazing thing they were doing. Starting a club just like the one their mothers had had, holding a meeting in the very same house in the very same town, even being watched over by the very same owl!

Cricket was thinking the same thing. "Go on," she urged. She wished they had a camera to record the moment. "It's been more than twenty-five years since the last meeting. No point in waiting any longer."

"All right then. Here goes!" Meg raised the gavel over her head and brought it down with a bang. "Hear yea, hear yea," she announced. "The Always Friends Club—the *new* Always Friends Club—is called to order." She banged two more times for good measure. "What should we do first?"

"The money!" Amy exclaimed, taking the words right out of Cricket's mouth. "Before we do anything else we should choose who gets to spend the money we earned by doing that focus group at the computer company last Saturday. Did everyone bring their twenty-five dollars?"

Cricket's heart suddenly beat faster. This was it. She thought of the box full of golden-colored puppies. Her dream was about to come true. Reaching into the pocket of her shirt, she pulled out the bills—two tens

23

and a five—that she'd gotten from the bank in exchange for the check the computer company had sent. They felt crisp and clean in her hand as she laid them at the owl's feet, on top of the five- and ten-dollar bills that Amy and Meg had taken from their pockets.

The stack wasn't high. It didn't look like much. But it was a lot of money. More money than any of the three girls had ever earned on her own.

"And this doesn't even include Brittany's," said Meg. "With hers there'll be one hundred dollars! Enough for a round-trip plane ticket from Los Angeles. That's what I'm going to buy if my name's chosen. I'll give it to my friend Jenny so she can come to visit over Christmas vacation."

"Well, I might get a good pair of Rollerblades or a tennis racket, if I win," said Amy. "Or maybe I'll just save the money for sports camp this summer. How about you?" She looked at Cricket.

"Me?" For a moment, Cricket was too over-whelmed by what she'd just heard Meg and Amy say-ing to speak. What was wrong with her? For the entire week, she'd been so focused on the puppies that she hadn't even thought about what plans the other girls might have for the money. Now, to hear them talking about Christmas vacation and summer camp—things that were months and months away—to think of Amy getting the money and locking it up in the bank while those ten little golden brown puppies went to other people's homes . . . It was just too much!

"Cricket?" said Meg. "Are you all right? You look sort of sick. Is that why you were late getting here?"

"No. No, I'm not sick," Cricket said quickly, recovering her voice. She suddenly realized that what with listening to Kevin's complaints and hearing about Brittany's riding lesson, and then climbing up here, she hadn't had a chance to tell them the news. "I was late because I was at the kennel," she said. "The puppies were born! Mrs. Wilson called this morning to tell me and I rushed right over there and . . . Oh, Meg, you've just got to see them. There are ten of them and they're all so cute! They've got the silkiest fur, and their faces are all wrinkled up like golden-colored raisins. Mrs. Wilson let me hold one and it was so soft and warm. She said if I want one I have to tell her soon because she's already got deposits on three of them. Cindy's puppies always go fast, she said. I have to give her one hundred dollars now and the rest later, but I told her that was no problem because I already have—"

She stopped, suddenly aware of the way the other girls were looking at her. "I mean, I hope I'll have . . . You see, I had a dream," she said, a note of desperation creeping into her voice. "There was this dog. It wasn't a puppy, it was a big dog, sort of shaggy and dirty. But I'm sure that it meant—"

Amy rolled her eyes. "A dream?" She knew all about Cricket's dreams and mysterious feelings. "But you can't depend on a dream coming true," she said. "We're drawing names from a hat, Cricket. It's a matter of chance."

"I know, but . . ." Cricket looked at the stack of bills lying at the owl's feet. She knew that Amy was right. She couldn't count on getting the money, but she couldn't bear to think of *not* getting it.

"I'll bet they really are cute," said Meg sympathetically. She exchanged a glance with Amy. They knew Cricket had been visiting the kennel every day for the past week. And they knew all about Cricket's dog, Pete, that had died. In fact, one of the first things Cricket had done when she met Meg was to show her Pete's grave in the Connors's backyard. But knowing all that didn't change anything. They still had to choose names from a hat.

"Look," said Amy suddenly, "let's just do it and get it over with. We can use this old hat." She climbed over a stack of magazines to retrieve the straw hat hanging from the deer antlers on the attic wall. "Meg, don't you need something from downstairs? Something that Cricket could get."

"What?" Meg said. Amy frowned at her. "Oh . . . oh, yes." She looked as if a light had gone on in her brain. "Cricket, how about going down to my room and getting . . . uh . . . a pencil and some paper from my desk. We'll need it to write our names on."

"But Meg . . ." Cricket began. She didn't like being ordered around, told to go fetch things like . . . well, like a dog. But this was no time to argue. She couldn't afford to waste a bit of energy because she had to wish as she'd never wished before. "All right, I'll go," she said. Heading for the trapdoor, she climbed down the stairway to Meg's room.

She found a pencil and some paper on the old wooden desk across from the bed. And she found something else, too. A tiny teddy bear, small enough to slip into a pocket, leaning against the base of the desk lamp. The bear was wearing a T-shirt with a heart drawn on it, and inside the heart were the words *Always Friends*.

Meg's friend Jenny had given Meg the bear. Cricket picked it up, marveling again at the way Jenny had written those words without knowing anything about the Always Friends Club. How could she, when Meg hadn't known anything about it herself yet!

It was a sign, Cricket was sure of it. It meant that she and Meg had been destined to meet, to find the attic, discover the scrapbook, and start the club. And maybe, she thought now, maybe it also meant the bear had special powers. Maybe it could bring me luck, just like it brought Meg luck in finding friends when she moved up here. She picked up the little teddy bear and slipped it into the pocket of her shirt. She was sure Meg wouldn't mind. Magic didn't wear out. Then, trying to visualize the bear radiating power all around her, she hurried back up the stairway to the attic.

Meg and Amy were whispering to each other, their heads close together, when Cricket appeared. But they moved quickly apart when they saw her.

"Oh, thank you," Meg said, her cheeks coloring

slightly as she took the pencil and paper from Cricket's hand. Not looking her in the eye, she tore the paper into four pieces. "Now, I'll write Brittany's name on one," she said. She printed BRITTANY on the paper in big bold letters, showed it to the other girls, then folded it up and dropped it in the hat. "You do the same with your name," she directed Cricket, handing her a piece of paper. "And Amy and I will do ours."

Cricket scarcely heard what she said. She didn't even care that the girls must have been talking about her when she came up the stairway. She was concentrating too hard to worry about that. Her fingers were so tense she could barely move the pencil, but she managed to print her name on the paper. Passing the pencil on to Amy, she folded up the paper and dropped it into the hat.

She closed her eyes, thinking of the powerful little bear in her pocket, of the golden-brown puppies cuddled up beside their mother in the big wooden box at the Sunny Hill Kennels. When she opened her eyes, Amy and Meg had dropped their papers into the hat, too.

"Okay. Who wants to pick?" asked Amy.

"You do it, Meg," Cricket said nervously, as Amy tossed the papers around in the hat and then held it up high. "I can't. I can't even look." She closed her eyes again as Meg reached into the hat.

"All right, here it is," she heard Meg say.

She opened her eyes. The paper was in Meg's hand.

It had to be hers. Please, please, please, she wished with every cell in her body.

"And the winner is . . ." Meg announced. She unfolded the paper and looked at the name. "Oh no," she said. She shot a disappointed glance at Amy. "It's Brittany!"

Chapter

3

Brittany? But she doesn't need it." The words were out of Cricket's mouth before she could stop them. "She's rich!"

"Well, that's not exactly true," said Meg. "Her parents are rich, but that doesn't mean—"

But Cricket was too upset to listen. "Even you and Amy don't need it," she rushed on. "At least not right away. You'll have plenty of time to earn money before Christmas, and even more time before summer. But Cindy's puppies . . ." Cricket could hardly say it. "Cindy's puppies will be gone!"

"Well, at least we tried," Amy said.

Something in her voice made Cricket stop. "What do you mean?" she asked.

Amy glanced at Meg. Then she dumped the remaining three papers out of the hat. "Look," she said, unfolding the papers and spreading them out on the footlocker.

CRICKET was printed on the first, CRICKET was printed on the second, and CRICKET was printed on the third.

Cricket stared at the papers. "But . . . but I don't understand. I only wrote my name on one. How could . . . Oh, no," she murmured as the truth dawned on her. "You mean you . . ." A lump suddenly rose in her throat. She couldn't go on.

"We know how much you want one of those puppies," said Meg.

"But . . . but you gave up your own chances," Cricket said, her voice choking up. "You shouldn't have done that."

"Oh, it wasn't all that noble," said Amy, who hated it when people started blubbering. "Christmas and summer *are* a long time from now, just like you said. We'll earn lots of money before then. We're not really giving up anything."

"But we couldn't decide for Brittany," said Meg. "We had to write in her name."

Cricket picked up the paper with Brittany's name on it. How close she had come. Four pieces of paper, three with her name, and *this* was the one that had been picked!

Her fingers closed around the paper. How easy it would be to crumple it up, to toss it away in a corner of the attic. She cast a cautious glance at the other girls. Were they thinking the same thing? Brittany wouldn't have to know. They would never have to tell.

"Cricket," Meg warned. "We can't—" But she was interrupted by a sudden shout from downstairs.

"Meg!" It was Kevin. "Meg," he yelled at the top of his lungs. "She's here. Brittany's here. Look out the window!"

Cricket dropped the paper.

Meg rushed to the attic window along with Amy. "She must have finished her riding lesson early," she said.

Cricket felt as if she'd just been jerked back from the edge of a cliff. She followed her friends to the window and got there just in time to see Brittany Logan stepping out of the back door of a sleek black limousine parked in the driveway.

"Oh my gosh, will you look at that," murmured Amy.

She didn't mean the limousine. They had seen that before. They'd seen the chauffeur in his dark blue uniform, too. But they hadn't seen Brittany in her riding outfit.

"She looks like she just stepped out of the pages of a book!" exclaimed Meg.

"*A Very Young Rider*," said Cricket, knowing exactly what book she meant. She remembered poring over the beautiful photographs of horses and riders. The book was part of a series—other books featured young dancers and young actresses—and Brittany could easily have starred in any of them. Momentarily speechless, the girls watched as she got out of the car.

Brittany's tawny blond hair, which usually tumbled over her shoulders, was pulled back into a neat bun at the nape of her neck. Her long slender legs were encased in close-fitting tan riding pants and black leather boots that came up to her knees. Her jacket, worn over a black turtleneck shirt, fit like it was made just for her, which undoubtedly it had been. An Adrienne Logan—her mother's—design, for sure. Instead of carrying a riding whip like the girl in the book, she held a large paper shopping bag in one hand. She leaned into the car to say something to the driver and then started up the walk to the house.

"Uh-oh, there's Kevin," said Meg, as her little brother appeared, racing down the walk toward Brittany. "I'd better go rescue her. And . . . and tell her that she won," she added quickly.

Her words hit Cricket like a splash of cold water. It was true then. There was no getting around it. The stack of bills lying at the owl's feet belonged to Brittany. And nothing Cricket might do—not even tearing the paper into a thousand pieces and swallowing it—could change that.

Meg gave Cricket a final sympathetic glance and then disappeared down the stairway. Amy picked up the paper with Brittany's name on it and smoothed it out. Cricket was grateful that she didn't try to say anything to cheer her up. She didn't think she could bear being told everything would be okay!

Meg had a hard time getting Brittany away from

Kevin. Cricket and Amy could hear his protests all the way from the bottom of the house to the top. They got louder as the girls entered Meg's room and headed for the attic.

"Now, Kevin, you can't come up here," Meg declared.

"But I want to see Brittany," he complained.

"Well, she has to see us first."

"Don't worry. I'll be down soon, Kevin," said Brittany, her voice sounding louder as she began climbing up the stairway. "Oh, this is so exciting!"

Cricket and Amy heard Kevin storm out of the closet and stomp across Meg's room.

"A secret stairway, a hidden attic. *C'est fantastique!*"

"I'll bet that means fantastic," Meg said, climbing up the stairway after Brittany.

"*Oui* . . . I mean, yes." Brittany, whose cheeks were already pink and glowing—probably from galloping around on that glistening black horse, Cricket thought—blushed as she always did when she got her languages confused. "Many words are almost the same in English and French," she explained.

Then she stepped out onto the attic floor, the shopping bag still in her hands. Her eyes—her beautiful blue, heavily lashed eyes—opened wide in amazement. "Oh, but this is wonderful!" she exclaimed. "Even better than you described it, Meg. I'm so glad I could come. I'm afraid that I lied, though," she added, grin-

34

ning at Amy and Cricket. "I told the riding teacher that my mother wanted me home early. Henry—that's the . . . the chauffeur—" She blushed again. "He's very nice, so he promised not to tell. He's gone to get gas, but he'll be back soon, so I can only stay a short while."

"And . . . and did Meg tell you?" Cricket asked, wanting to get it over with.

"About the money? Yes!" Brittany's face glowed as Amy took the stack of bills from the footlocker and handed them to her. "I can hardly believe it," she said, not seeming to notice the expression on Cricket's face. "I've never won anything. Though this isn't really winning, I suppose. It's choosing. Anyway, I know exactly what I'm going to do with it. I saw a wonderful camera in a store downtown. I'm going to buy it so we can take pictures for the club! And look—"

She stuffed the money into her jacket pocket and opened the shopping bag she was carrying. "I already bought this with my allowance." She pulled out an enormous scrapbook. It had a pale pink cover with a pattern of bright pink and red hearts. "We can put photos and souvenirs from our projects in it," she said enthusiastically. "We can make a scrapbook just like the original club kept. And just wait until you see the camera. It has a zoom lens and a built-in flash and—" Suddenly she stopped. "But what am I talking about?" she said, blushing again. "If I was chosen, that means the rest of you weren't. That seems so unfair!"

"No, it's not," said Meg quickly. "We'll all have a

chance. That's the point of the club, isn't it?" She looked at Cricket.

"Uh . . . yes," Cricket said. She could hardly say no. Not with everyone staring at her. Why was Brittany being so nice anyway? Buying a scrapbook with her own allowance, getting a camera that the whole club could use. It made it hard to hate her, which was what Cricket wished she could do!

"Well, that's good," said Brittany, looking relieved. "Because I wouldn't want anyone to feel . . . I mean, I think it's important that we all . . ."

"Brittany, stop worrying!" said Amy. "The camera sounds like a great idea. If we're going to be in a club together we can't be saying we're sorry about things all the time. We have to be like a family. My brothers *never* apologize to me! I'll bet the girls in the original club didn't waste time like that, either. Here. Just look at all the things they did." She took the new scrapbook from Brittany and handed her the old one. "They wouldn't have been able to do half of this stuff if they'd wasted time worrying."

Brittany opened the scrapbook. "I've been wanting to see this," she said. Cricket had a feeling she was making an effort not to apologize for apologizing! She sat down on the lounge chair cushion with the scrapbook in her lap, stretching her shiny black boots out in front of her.

"I wish I could take these off," she said. "But you know riding boots. They're so hard to get back on!"

"Uh . . . yes," said Meg, who didn't know any such thing. She cast an anxious glance at Cricket, who was staring enviously at the tight black boots.

"I hate getting dressed up like this," Brittany went on. "But my mother insisted. We always wore outfits like this in France when we rode. But next time I'm wearing jeans and a sweatshirt. Oh, look . . ." She leaned over the scrapbook eagerly. "They decorated the pages with drawings and borders. I think we should do that with ours. And here are their goals. 'To have fun, to help people, to earn money, and to always be friends,'" she read from the minutes taped to the first page. "I think we should make them our goals, too."

"Especially the part about having fun!" agreed Amy. "That sounds good to me. I don't think we should do any projects that are dreary. Like washing dishes. I get enough of that at home!"

"I agree," said Meg, glad to have a chance to shift attention from Brittany's riding clothes. "But I think the helping people part is important, too. I was talking to my mom about it just last night. She said that we can't expect to make money on all our projects, but that if we manage to help people, then at least we'll have accomplished something we can be proud of."

"Well, I think the most important part is about always being friends," said Brittany, looking up from the scrapbook. "Friendship is the most important thing in the world. More important than money, more important than helping people even. Why if I hadn't met all of you . . ."

Her voice filled with emotion. "I don't know what would have happened. You're the best thing that ever—"

Cricket couldn't stand it. "Stop it, Brittany!" she exclaimed. "Stop being so . . . so nice!"

Brittany leaped to her feet. "Cricket, what's wrong? What did I say? I didn't mean to—"

"She's upset," Meg said quickly. "You see she wanted—"

"Don't say it!" Cricket warned. She was not going to have Meg telling Brittany about Cindy's puppies. She was not going to have Brittany feeling sorry for her. Brittany would probably reach into her pocket and hand over the money. But Cricket didn't want it like that. Not if it meant she'd have to be grateful forever to Brittany Logan! "I'm all right." She shrugged off the hand Meg had placed on her shoulder. "I just . . ." But she couldn't think of any way to explain her behavior.

Luckily, Amy came to her rescue. "Look, maybe we should stop all this talk and just choose someone to come up with our next project," she said. "I'm going to have to go to soccer practice soon and Brittany's probably going to have to leave, too."

"Good idea," said Meg, eager to smooth things over. She took a sheet of paper and began tearing it into pieces.

Brittany looked at Cricket uneasily. "Well, if you're sure you're all right . . ." she said. She took the pencil Meg held out to her and wrote her name on a piece of paper.

38

Cricket struggled to pull herself together. The way she felt now, she didn't even care if there was a next project. And she certainly didn't care who came up with it. But she couldn't let Meg and Amy down. Trying to look as if nothing had happened, she took the pencil Brittany passed to her, wrote her name on a piece of paper, and dropped it into the hat.

Meg and Amy did the same. When all the names were in—and Cricket was sure there were four different ones this time—Amy held the hat up high. "Who wants to choose?" she asked. "Cricket?"

Cricket didn't want to, but she couldn't say no. Not with Brittany standing there looking at her as if she were some kind of lunatic ready to crack at any moment. "All right," she agreed, forcing the corners of her mouth up in what she hoped was a cheerful smile. She reached into the hat. Her fingers grasped one of the papers and pulled it out just as a car horn honked outside.

"Oh, I'll bet that's Henry with the car," Brittany said, running to the window. "I told him to just honk."

Meg's mother appeared at the bottom of the attic stairway. "Brittany, you have to go," she called. "And Amy, maybe you'd better go, too. Your mother told me to be sure you left for practice on time."

"I could give you a lift," offered Brittany.

"In the limousine?" Amy dropped the hat. "Oh, I'd love that!" she exclaimed, looking as if Brittany had offered her a ride on the space shuttle. "I'm dying to see what it's like."

"Well, this may be your last chance," said Brittany. "My father's company leased it for him for just a month and the month's up next weekend. Come on." She started for the stairway, then stopped. "Wait! What's the matter with me? The name," she said, turning to Cricket uncertainly. "Whose did you pick?"

Cricket unfolded the paper. She stared at the name. "Oh, no. I don't believe it," she said. Now she knew how Cinderella must have felt when her stepsisters got invited to the ball and she got invited to scrub the scullery. "It's mine." She held out the paper with her name printed on it. "You get the money, Brittany, and I get the work!"

Chapter

I still can't believe I said that!" Cricket slumped over the kitchen table, her freckled face buried in her hands. A plate full of her mother's miniature cheese tarts, which Mrs. Kelly had heated in the oven, lay untasted on the table in front of her. "What am I? A monster? A self-centered, green-eyed monster?"

"No," Meg said loyally. "Of course not. You were just a little upset."

"Upset? Oh, Meg, I was crazy!" Cricket exclaimed. She raked her fingers through her curly red hair, making it stand out around her head like a carrot-colored halo. "I wasn't thinking of anyone but myself. Brittany didn't do anything wrong. She was being nice. Too nice, maybe, but still . . . Oh, Meg, I don't know," she groaned. "Maybe I don't belong in this club!"

"Don't say that. Of course you do," Meg insisted, reaching across the table to squeeze her hand. "You made a mistake, but you apologized."

That was true. Almost as soon as the words were out of Cricket's mouth, she'd said she was sorry—not once, but twice (in spite of Amy's prohibition). But she could never forget the look on Brittany's face— stunned, hurt, as if she'd been slapped. It was just like the time she'd lost her temper with Pete because he gnawed the head off one of her Madame Alexander dolls. She'd flown off the handle and hit him right on his soft black nose. Of course, she'd immediately thrown her arms around his neck and burst into tears and Pete had licked her all over her face and whim- pered sympathetically as if *she* were the one who'd been hit. But it had been weeks before he'd really trusted her again. She was afraid it would be the same with Brittany. Only worse. You couldn't win people over with dog biscuits!

"Could I say something?" said Mrs. Kelly. She was at the stove, stirring a pot of soup she was heating for lunch. "I know that you're feeling bad right now. And probably Brittany is, too. But I think it's good that you girls are getting these things ironed out right at the start. When your mother and I had our club, Cricket, we tried so hard to be nice that by the time we'd done four or five projects, everyone was full of resentments. You know those pictures in the scrapbook of us cele- brating Karen's birthday?"

Cricket nodded. She loved those pictures of her mother's birthday party. Everyone in the club was smiling and looked so happy. Not like pictures of their club would look if they took them right now.

"Well," Mrs. Kelly went on, "right after those pictures were taken, everything fell apart. We started talking about the club, and in no time we were accusing each other of not working hard enough and of coming up with stupid ideas for projects. In no time at all we were having a food fight. Most of that beautiful birthday cake wound up on the wall!"

"No kidding!" said Meg, looking at her mother with a mixture of surprise and admiration.

"What's this about birthday cake?" Her grandfather appeared at the kitchen door. He was carrying Kevin on his shoulders. He'd taken him out to the backyard to look for a woodpecker nest in one of the pine trees, hoping that it would make him forget about Brittany leaving. It seemed to have worked.

"I want birthday cake," Kevin said now, every bit as insistently as he'd once said, "I want Brittany."

Mrs. Kelly shook her head. "Kevin, you are too much," she said. "I'm afraid we don't have any cake, but we have these cheese tarts that Cricket's mother made. No one's tried them yet. And I'll be dishing up this soup in a minute."

"Ah, good!" said Meg's grandmother as she came into the kitchen. She'd been working on the computer in the den. "I'm starved!" She gave Meg and Cricket each a squeeze.

Cricket liked the way Meg's grandmother

43

smelled—sort of like roses and wool sweaters. And suddenly she felt better. Maybe Meg's mother was right about the club. They were just getting started after all. They couldn't expect everything to go smoothly. Maybe she could come up with a really terrific project—something that would be lots of fun and that would earn a hundred dollars for each of them!

"I hear you're going to be the idea girl this time, Cricket," Meg's grandmother said, sitting down at the table beside her. "If you want my advice, don't think up anything that requires a computer! I've spent all morning trying to figure out how to do merge printing and I still don't get it. You should tell that company of yours to hire someone to write better manuals, Janet," she said to Meg's mother.

"Yes, Mom," Mrs. Kelly replied, sounding as if she'd been told to floss her teeth before going to bed. "I'll do that. Now let's forget about projects. I want everyone to try the tarts. Karen said she wanted our opinion."

"Well, if Cricket's mother made them, I'm sure they're delicious," said Meg's grandfather, stooping down so Kevin could slide off his shoulders and onto a chair. "Her recipes certainly have done wonders for my cooking."

Meg and Cricket exchanged a glance. Cricket could see that Meg was trying to keep a straight face, but she couldn't keep her eyes from smiling mischievously. And for the first time since she'd exploded at

Brittany—no, for the first time since Brittany's name had been pulled from the hat—Cricket found herself smiling, too. Because although Meg's grandfather loved to cook, before Mrs. Connors had started helping him, all his dishes—which were super-healthy, heavy on the bean sprouts and tofu—had been terrible to eat.

Kevin had become very suspicious about food. "What are those green things?" he asked now, eyeing the tiny chunks that dotted the filling of the tarts. He looked at Cricket accusingly.

"I'm not sure, Kevin," she replied. "I didn't watch my mom making them. I was too busy getting ready to—" She stopped herself before she could say "go to the kennel." She didn't want to start thinking about Cindy's puppies again. At least not yet. "I know she made lots for a wedding this afternoon," she went on. "She said they were a new recipe she'd just made up." She looked at the tarts warily now, too. What *were* those green things?

"It's too bad Amy and Brittany are missing out," said Mrs. Kelly. "I should have heated these up right away. But maybe we can save a few."

"Not likely," said Meg's grandfather, passing the plate around. "If these are half as good as her usual creations, there won't be any left." He put the plate down, took one of the tarts for himself, and bit into it.

Cricket did the same. She chewed. A sour taste exploded in her mouth, followed by something hot— very hot! "Uh . . . ooh . . ." she gasped. "Water!"

Kevin, who had crammed an entire tart into his mouth, wrinkled up his face as though he'd bitten into a cactus and spit the tart onto the table. "Yuck!" he cried, tears starting to run down his cheeks. "That hurt!" His mother quickly filled a glass with water and handed it to him. Kevin gulped it down as she passed another glass to Cricket.

Meg's grandfather blinked, swallowed, then took off his glasses and wiped his eyes. "Well," he said. "That was . . . interesting."

Meg dropped the tart she was holding. Her grandmother picked it up and broke it apart. She extracted one of the green things and tasted it. "Why, it's a pickle," she said. "A very sour pickle. And this—" She picked out a small green chunk, a shade darker, and tasted it gingerly with the tip of her tongue. "This is a chili pepper—one of those little green ones they use in Thai food, I think." She fanned her mouth with her hand. "How about sharing some of that water, Kevin," she said.

Mrs. Kelly and Meg tried a tiny bit of tart next, but each of them quickly reached for the water, too. "My goodness," said Mrs. Kelly. "Whatever could she have been thinking?"

"Maybe she bought the wrong kind of chilies," suggested Meg. "Some kinds aren't this hot."

"But that doesn't explain the pickles," her mother pointed out.

Cricket didn't know what to say. She wasn't as surprised as the others were by the tarts. Actually, except for the chilies being so hot, they were a lot better tasting than the anchovy omelet her mother had served up for dinner last night. The odd thing was that she'd thought it was good. She hadn't been able to understand why Cricket and her father wouldn't eat it.

"Mom's been kind of stressed out lately," she said, searching for an explanation. "Maybe it's affected her tastebuds. She's had a lot of orders to fill and she's been pretty tired, too. She starts yawning around eight o'clock. Last night she went to bed before me!"

"Really?" Mrs. Kelly frowned. "Strange tastes in food, sleepiness . . ." She exchanged a look with Meg's grandmother. "Does she have any other symptoms?" she asked.

"Symptoms?" Cricket didn't like the sound of that word. Symptoms were what you told your doctor about. "Why? Do you think there's something wrong with her?" she asked.

"No, of course not," Mrs. Kelly replied quickly. Perhaps too quickly. She exchanged another glance with Meg's grandmother and then whisked the plate of tarts from the table and began ladling out bowls of soup. "Even the best of cooks can have a bad day," she said.

"I can attest to that!" agreed Meg's grandfather cheerfully. "Now eat up, girls. Then Kevin and I will take you out in the backyard and show you that woodpecker's nest."

47

Normally Cricket, who liked all kinds of animals, would have been interested, but not now. Too many things were going through her mind. "I'll pass on the nest. And on the soup, too," she said, pushing her chair back from the table. "I think I'd better get home." She thanked Meg's mother, who tried to persuade her to stay, and headed quickly out the door.

Meg ran after her. "Cricket, wait!" she called, catching up with her just as she reached her bike. "Don't worry about your mom. I'm sure there's nothing wrong with her."

"But she has been awfully tired," Cricket said, realizing all at once that she really *was* worried. "Absentminded, too. And then there's the food . . ."

"Well, maybe she just needs a good night's sleep," said Meg. "My mom will call her. She'll find out what's going on. Don't be like me and let your imagination run away with you. And don't worry about Brittany, either," she added. "All you have to do is come up with a great project that we can all have fun doing and everything will be fine."

"Sure," said Cricket, trying to sound more confident than she felt. She swung her leg over the seat of her bike and coasted out of the driveway. "If you have any ideas, give me a call. I'll need all the help I can get!"

That was an understatement. The truth was, Cricket hadn't given any thought to what the club might do next. She'd been too busy thinking about the puppies.

Though she tried not to, she couldn't help thinking about them again. She wanted to steer her bike straight up the street that led to the kennels. She wanted to race right in and tell Mrs. Wilson that she'd have the deposit for her in no time—maybe by next week, when the club had carried out the terrific project she was going to think up. But she didn't. After all, even if they earned the money her name might not be picked. She turned her bike resolutely down the street leading toward home. She wasn't stupid. She wasn't about to make the same mistake twice. If she'd learned anything it was that you shouldn't count on money you didn't already have!

Of course, there was one other possibility. Her parents. They knew she wanted a dog. They'd talked at one time about paying for half. But that had been before they'd started having so many expenses, like the water heater that had to be replaced, and the clutch that went out on the car, and the roof that leaked. Cricket had heard them talking about it. "Why does everything have to come at once?" her mother had sighed. "The only way we're going to be able to manage all this is if we don't spend anything extra for at least a year!"

Still . . . her father *was* fixing the roof by himself. That should save something. And they'd already paid for the water heater and the clutch on the car. Cricket felt her hopes rising as she turned into her block and headed for the Connors's small wood frame house— blue with white trim and a bright yellow door. A red truck with black writing on the side—Redwood Grove Roofing—was parked at the curb in front of the house. Her father and a man wearing jeans and a work shirt were standing in the driveway, looking up at the roof and talking.

"Cricket," her father said as she swung into the drive and leaped from her bike, "I'd like you to meet Mr. Miller. We're going to be sending him to Hawaii for Christmas. And maybe paying for his kids' college education, too."

"Very funny, Mr. Connors," said Mr. Miller, smiling as if he were used to such jokes and didn't mind them at all. He climbed into his truck. "We'll be here a week from Wednesday," he said, starting the engine. "Let's hope it doesn't rain before then."

Mr. Connors watched him go. "What a cheerful man," he said, smiling wryly. "And why wouldn't he be? He's got one of the best jobs in town—especially with the rainy season coming on."

"Dad, does this mean you couldn't fix the roof yourself?" Cricket felt her hopes sinking.

"That's exactly what it means," replied Mr. Connors. "I'm afraid that keeping a roof over our heads—at least a roof that won't leak—is going to cost a fortune. Well, a fortune to us, anyway." He looked at Cricket seriously. "You went to the kennel today, didn't you?" he said. "Mom told me the owner called to say those puppies were born."

Cricket nodded. She started to speak, then stopped

herself. She had a feeling this wasn't the best time to tell her dad about how wonderful the puppies were and how soon Mrs. Wilson needed to have a deposit.

Her father sighed and looked up at the roof again. "Listen, Cricket," he said. "I've been thinking. You know the county animal shelter? They've got some wonderful dogs there who really need good homes; and—" He stopped, seeing the look in Cricket's eyes. "Well, we can talk about it later," he said quickly. "Right now I've got to take the shingles I bought back to the lumberyard and see if I can get a refund." He climbed into his old VW bus, which was parked in the drive behind Mrs. Connors's catering van. "But think about it," he said as he started the engine. "You'd be doing a really good deed."

Chapter

5

Cricket watched her father pull out of the driveway. A dog from the shelter? How could he think that after seeing Cindy's puppies, after holding one in her hands, she would ever . . . She was not going to think about it. She knew her father loved her. She knew he wanted the best for her, but this time he was wrong!

Cricket put her bike in the garage, went into the house, and headed straight for her favorite room—the kitchen. It was bright and cheery with posters of vegetables and fruits on the walls and gleaming copper pots hanging above the big white double-oven stove. There was lots of counter space and all kinds of cooking equipment—a mixer, food processor, pasta maker, blender, plus lots of knives, wire whisks, and wooden spoons in all shapes and sizes.

Usually, some wonderful aroma was coming from the oven or from a pot on the stove. But today, an acrid, burning smell hung in the air. Cricket's mother was talking on the phone at the counter that divided the cooking area from the breakfast nook she used as an office.

"Yes," she was saying. "I understand. You're quite right." She waved to Cricket and pointed at the receiver, rolling her eyes and making a face like a mournful circus clown.

Cricket peered into the sink at a blackened pot half-filled with water. The charred remains of what looked like marbles made out of volcanic lava had been dumped in the trash. Wrinkling her nose at the smell, she took a seat on a stool at the counter. Without thinking, she reached for one of the green-speckled tarts piled on a platter in front of her. She was about to take a bite when she suddenly realized it was one of the same tarts she'd tasted at Meg's house.

"A full refund. Of course," Mrs. Connors said into the phone, as Cricket dropped the tart back onto the plate. "And I'm terribly sorry. I can assure you it won't—" She held the receiver away from her ear. Cricket could hear angry words and then a bang as the receiver at the other end of the line was slammed down.

"Well, I guess that's that," her mother sighed, hanging the phone back on the wall. "I don't think Mrs. Simon will be recommending me to any of her friends who are putting on weddings."

She sank down on a stool at the counter. "A full

refund," she groaned, running her fingers through her hair, which was curly and red just like Cricket's. "All that work, all those ingredients—a total loss!" She stared at the plate of tarts. "And I thought they were so good," she said. "A little different maybe, but . . . Did you taste them? What did Meg's mother and the other girls think?"

Cricket decided this was no time to spare her mom's feelings. She'd already been yelled at by a customer. It was better that she know the truth so she'd never make the recipe again. "Mom, they were awful," she said bluntly. "Nobody could eat them. What were you thinking of when you made them?"

"I don't know." Mrs. Connors shook her head. "I burned the cocktail meatballs I was making for the Watkins party tonight, too. I just wandered out into the backyard while they were browning. I noticed the roses needed pruning, so I got the shears and . . . well, I completely forgot about the meatballs! I don't know what's wrong with me. Am I losing my mind or something?"

"Mom, don't say that!" Cricket reached across the counter to touch her mother's hand. "There's nothing wrong with you, you're just . . ." But she didn't know what to say. "Have you ever felt like this before?" she asked, the worries she'd set aside coming back to her. "I mean, forgetful, having strange tastes, getting sleepy. You have been awfully sleepy lately, Mom," she said.

Mrs. Connors frowned. "I guess I have been all those things, haven't I?" she said. "But I've never . . . well, except for when—" She stopped. A peculiar expression came over her face.

"Mom, what is it?" said Cricket.

"Oh. Oh, nothing," Mrs. Connors replied. "It's just that—" She was interrupted by the sudden ringing of the phone. "Oh dear, I hope this isn't another angry customer," she said, as she picked up the receiver. But it wasn't. It was Meg's mother. "Oh, Janet!" Mrs. Connors said, sounding relieved. "Yes. We were just talking about those tarts. I'm so sorry, I don't know what I—Yes. Yes, that's right, I have been. Any other symptoms? Well—" She shot a quick glance at Cricket, who was hanging on every word. "Wait a second, Janet," she said. "I'm going to take this on the other phone." She held out the receiver to Cricket. "Could you hang this up after I've picked up the phone in the bedroom?" she asked.

Cricket nodded. Not that she wanted to hang up the phone. What she wanted to do was press her ear against the receiver and listen to every single word. But she couldn't do that. Her mother didn't eavesdrop on her conversations, after all.

"You can hang up now, Cricket," Mrs. Connors called when she reached the bedroom.

Cricket stretched for the phone rest fastened to the wall. The mothers had already started talking. She wasn't listening, not intentionally, but she couldn't help hearing one of them saying something about giving up hope.

She caught her breath. Giving up hope. That was what the vet had said when she and her dad had taken Pete to his animal clinic for the very last time. "I hate giving up hope . . ." Those had been his very words. "But it doesn't look good." And where was Pete now? In a grave in the Connors's backyard, that's where!

"Mom," Cricket said anxiously when her mother returned to the kitchen, "is anything wrong? What did Meg's mother say?"

"I hope you weren't listening," said Mrs. Connors. She didn't look sick, Cricket noticed, just sort of distracted.

"Of course not! I only want to know—"

"Oh, Cricket, there's nothing to know." Mrs. Connors gave her a squeeze. "Nothing to worry about, either. You should be thinking of your club. Meg's mother said you'd been chosen to come up with the next project. Now let me see. Maybe you could do something with cooking. I've got lots of equipment you could use. And plenty of experience. I could be your consultant."

"Yes, but—" Cricket could tell her mother was trying to distract her.

"Maybe you could make chocolate chip cookies to sell at one of Amy's soccer games," Mrs. Connors rushed on, ignoring her interruption. "Or fruitcakes for Christmas. Or you could wash something. Lots of things need washing. Like cars. Or kitchen walls. Now, that's a good project! No one likes to wash their kitchen walls."

Cricket hadn't even known that people washed walls. She could see why they wouldn't like it. But it didn't sound like something that would meet the club's goal of having fun!

"But Mom, before I think about projects, I want to know—" she began. Then she stopped. Suddenly she wasn't sure she really *did* want to know. Her mother said there was nothing to worry about. Why not just accept that? She didn't want to think about anything being wrong. She wanted to think about puppies and chocolate chips. "How many cookies would we have to bake to earn one hundred dollars?" she asked, shoving the phone conversation out of her mind.

Her mother looked relieved. "Well, that would depend on a lot of things," she said. "Like how big the cookies are and what you put in them. You'll have to subtract the cost of your ingredients to figure out how much profit you're actually making. I'll be glad to help you with it later," she said. "Right now, though, I've got to go to the market and get some more ground beef for those meatballs." She took her purse from a hook near the door. "I'm going to make a great dinner, too. Beef stroganoff! With no strange ingredients, I promise." And with that, she sailed out the door, whistling a tune from *The Sound of Music*. She certainly didn't sound like someone who'd given up hope!

Maybe I didn't hear right, Cricket thought. Maybe what she'd said was "starting to cope" or "trying not to mope." That's not bad advice for anyone. She decided to take it herself by sliding off her stool and finding one of her mother's favorite cookbooks—*The Joy of Cooking*—on the bookshelf in the pantry. She turned to the index at the back, found the heading "Cookies," and beneath that "Chocolate chip."

She sat down at the desk in the breakfast nook, where her mother did the paperwork for her business, and flipped through the pages of the cookbook. The recipe was short, and it looked pretty simple. She found a pencil and a notepad and began to list the ingredients they'd need: butter, brown sugar, white sugar, flour, baking soda, and chocolate chips, of course. Nuts, the recipe said, were optional.

But how much of each ingredient would they need? The recipe was for forty-five two-inch cookies, but a two-inch cookie didn't seem very big. Not for hungry kids at a soccer game. Four or five inches would be better, like those big chewy cookies they sold at Sweet Temptations, the best bakery in town. How much would they need to bake cookies like those? Should they double the recipe, triple it, or maybe quadruple it? And what would all this stuff cost? Even without the nuts, Cricket figured, it would be pretty expensive. She stared at the notepad, suddenly realizing what her mom went through every day with her business. It wasn't just cooking she did, it was math. No wonder she was so tired!

She looked up from the paper and stared absent-mindedly at the calendar above the desk. Her mother's business engagements and Cricket's school events were marked with red ink. At least they wouldn't have to worry about refunds, she thought. People at the soccer game next Saturday weren't likely to want their money back. But what was that? She leaned closer to the calendar.

"Oh no!" she groaned. For there, plainly marked on the calendar, was the soccer game. Only it wasn't next Saturday, as she'd thought, it was the Saturday after—two whole weeks away! She couldn't afford to wait that long. Not when people were so eager to reserve Cindy's puppies, and when it looked like she couldn't count on her parents for the deposit. She—or rather the club—had to start earning money soon.

Quickly, she flipped back to the index in the cookbook. What else had her mother suggested? Fruitcake. She ran her fingers through the Fs—frankfurters, fritters, frog legs. But fruitcake wouldn't do, either, she realized. No one would want one until Christmas! She slammed the book shut and stared out the window. Finding a project they could do soon was going to be harder than she'd thought!

By dinnertime, Cricket wasn't any closer to coming up with an idea than she'd been when she rode home from Meg's house. She thought of making jewelry. She'd made some great necklaces out of glazed beads in the summer art class she'd taken at the recreation center. Or maybe they could decorate shirts with lots of unusual buttons. She'd made a terrific-looking shirt for herself using a ton of old buttons from her mother's button box. But making things like that took time. And besides, once they had made them, where would they sell them?

Her head was beginning to ache from thinking so hard and it was a relief to sit down at the big round table in the dining room and taste the beef stroganoff her mother had cooked. It was delicious—no pickles, no chili peppers, and not the least bit burned. It was her dad's favorite dish, which might be why he looked at her mother so fondly all through the meal and leaped up so quickly to clear the table when it was over. Mrs. Connors, who'd been so busy with the meatballs and the stroganoff that she hadn't had time to help Cricket think about projects, was already yawning, though it was only seven-thirty.

"Why don't you go to bed now, honey," Mr. Connors said, giving her a hug. "Cricket and I will clean up in the kitchen."

"That sounds lovely," said Mrs. Connors, yawning again. "I really am sleepy."

Cricket's worries returned. "Dad," she said seriously, the moment her mother had disappeared into the bedroom, "is Mom all right?"

"Of course," Mr. Connors replied quickly. Too quickly, Cricket thought, remembering how eager Meg's mother had been to assure her of the same thing earlier in the day. "Everything's fine. Take my word for it. Have I ever misled you?"

Cricket shook her head, because he hadn't. Not yet.

"Then trust me," he said. "Mom's going to be fine."

It wasn't until later, much later, after Cricket had helped with the dishes, watched one of her favorite movies, *The Parent Trap,* on TV, and was in her room getting ready for bed that she thought about those words—*going to be fine*. That wasn't quite the same as saying, "Yes, your mom is fine," was it?

She took off her vest, unbuttoned her polka-dotted shirt, and tossed them on a chair. Something fell out of the pocket. Meg's bear! She'd forgotten all about it. She stooped down and picked it up, hoping that Meg hadn't missed it. She'd return it to her at school, but meanwhile maybe it could help. Not that it had done much good up until now, Cricket thought, setting it on her night table. But maybe its powers worked in strange ways. Maybe it could help make sure her mother was fine, not just "going to be fine." Or maybe it could help her think up a project.

She pulled off her tights and put on one of the oversized T-shirts she used for pajamas. Then she crawled into bed, pulling her comforter, covered with pictures of ladybugs and butterflies, up under her chin. Maybe her brain would work on things during the night. She'd heard that scientists often thought about problems they were trying to solve before falling asleep. They asked themselves questions and in the morning they woke up with the answers, just like magic. If it worked for them, then why not for her?

She closed her eyes. What do people want besides chocolate chip cookies? she asked. What do they need washed besides their kitchen walls? Her comforter felt warm and snug. She thought of the ladybugs crawling over it. She thought of the dream she'd had last night about the big shaggy dog. She remembered its muddy paws, its dirty white fur. And suddenly, her eyes popped open. That was it. Her dream *had* meant something. And she knew exactly what the club's next project would be!

Chapter

A dog washing service? Cricket, that's brilliant!" Meg's voice came out of the receiver so loudly that Cricket had to hold the phone away from her ear. "How did you ever think of it?"

"I didn't *think* of it. I *dreamed* it!" said Cricket. Meg's reaction was even better than she'd hoped for. She flopped back on her bed, the living room telephone, which had an extra long cord, in her hand. It was early. Very early. The morning light had just begun to filter through her window, but she hadn't been able to wait. Though she'd been afraid everyone in Meg's house would be asleep, she just had to call. Luckily, as Meg quickly assured her, families with four-year-old boys didn't sleep late, not even on Sundays.

"Amy's going to have to eat her words," Cricket said now. "She's always teasing me about thinking that my dreams mean something, but this time . . ." She described her dream to Meg, telling her about the shaggy dog and how it had put its paws on her shoulders and licked her face, how it had romped through the Connors's garden and rolled on their sofa with its dirty white fur. "I thought it was an omen telling me that I was going to *get* a dog," she said. "That's why I was so sure my name would be picked out of the hat yesterday. But what it really meant was that we were going to be *washing* dogs. That's why the dog in my dream was so big and dirty, not a sweet little puppy, like Cindy's."

Meg tended to be skeptical about Cricket's dreams, just as Amy was, but she had to admit this one seemed like more than just chance. "Maybe it is a good sign," she said. "In any case, the idea of a dog wash is terrific. I'm sure we'll get lots of customers. People need their dogs washed but they always put off doing it. Or else they take them to a dog groomer who charges a lot of money. We can cut the price and do just as good a job. It'll be like those car washes that high school kids are always putting on to raise money for band uniforms or the football team. But where can we hold it?"

"At my house next Saturday," said Cricket, who'd barely slept a wink last night thinking about it. "My parents are still asleep, so I haven't asked them yet, but I'm sure they won't mind. We've got a big laundry room and a huge tub where we used to bathe Pete. I think we even have some of his dog shampoo left." She was surprised to discover that for the first time since

Pete had died she didn't feel sad talking about him. *That* was a good sign, too.

"But how about . . ." Meg's voice sounded hesitant. "How about your mother? Is she—"

"She's fine," said Cricket, echoing her father but leaving out the "going to be" part. She didn't want to think about her mother. Not now.

Meg seemed to understand. "Good," she said, quickly dropping the subject. "Listen, I have to go now. I took the phone into the bathroom and Kevin's pounding on the door. Can you hear him?"

"Is that what it is?" Cricket had been wondering about the steady thumping sound she heard in the background. "I guess he really needs to get in there," she said. Meg had better go before Kevin had an accident! "Why don't we talk about all this after school tomorrow? We can have a planning meeting at Elmer's." Elmer's Ice Cream Emporium was a Redwood Grove institution. The original Always Friends Club had met there, and the girls had celebrated the formation of the new club there, too.

"Good idea," agreed Meg. "I always think better with a little ice cream in my stomach. I'll call Amy and tell her, but—" She hesitated. Cricket knew what she was going to say. "Maybe you should call Brittany."

"You're right. If we're going to work together . . ." Cricket's voice trailed off. She thought about the look on Brittany's face when she'd yelled at her in the attic.

Would Brittany believe her if she said that she was *really, really* sorry? She wanted to ask Meg what she should say, but the pounding on the bathroom door was getting louder and Meg had to hang up.

Cricket sat up on her bed and put the phone on the floor. The Connors's house was quiet. Too quiet, she sometimes thought. Kevin might annoy Meg, he might get into her stuff and bother her friends, but he certainly livened things up! She glanced at her Betty Boop clock. It was eight now, but that still seemed too early to call the Logans's house. People who drove around in limousines probably slept late. They probably had breakfast in bed, served on silver trays by a butler!

Not that Sunday breakfast at the Connors's house was anything to sneeze at. Cricket's dad usually did the cooking. This morning he whipped up his famous banana nut waffles, a steaming mug of hot chocolate for Cricket, and frothy cups of cappuccino for himself and Mrs. Connors. Cricket dug in hungrily. She'd worked up an appetite by waking up so early, and now she was so busy eating and talking about her plans, that she hardly noticed when her mother, suddenly looking pale, excused herself halfway through her waffle and rushed to the bathroom.

Her father cleared his throat. "Well, Cricket, that's great," he said heartily, as if to make certain she didn't notice that her mother was gone. "I think a dog washing service is an excellent idea. And you can certainly use the laundry room. I'll even chip in and buy you some flea soap. How are you going to advertise?" he asked.

Cricket hadn't thought about that. "I'm not sure," she said. "But we're having a meeting at Elmer's tomorrow after school. We'll figure out everything then."

"Good. Plenty of planning is the key to success," said Mr. Connors. "That, and getting the word out about your business. If I were you, I'd put up a notice at the animal shelter. Plenty of people would see it there. I'll be glad to drive you over anytime you want. While you're there, you could take a look at the dogs that are up for adoption," he added.

Cricket took that as her signal to leave. She'd finished her waffle and she did *not* want to sit around talking with her dad about dogs at the shelter. "I just remembered," she said, jumping up from the table. "I've got to call Brittany and tell her about the meeting." Taking the phone with her, she ducked into her room.

Brittany's phone number was written on a piece of paper tacked to Cricket's bulletin board, along with the numbers of the other girls in the club. Since Brittany had moved to Redwood Grove only a few weeks ago, Cricket had never called her before. She didn't know what to expect. Would a butler with a British accent come on the line and say, "Logan residence," in a formal-sounding voice, like in the movies? Or would Mrs. Logan—Adrienne Logan, the famous fashion designer—answer the phone and start speaking French?

Looking at the number, Cricket picked up the phone and dialed. The phone on the other end of the line began to ring. What should I say? she thought. Should I introduce myself? Are you supposed to introduce yourself to a butler? Should I say, "May I speak to Brittany?" Or should I say, "Is Brittany there?" She was relieved, but a bit disappointed, when the phone was picked up and Brittany herself said, "Hello."

"Brittany? It's me," Cricket said. "I mean, it's Cricket. I just . . ." She hesitated. Now that they were face to face—or phone to phone—she couldn't think of how to begin. "I'm sorry" sounded so lame, and besides she'd already said it. She wished she could just tell her about the meeting at Elmer's and hang up. But she had to say more. She couldn't just ignore what had happened yesterday. Luckily, Brittany didn't give her a chance.

"Cricket!" she exclaimed. "Oh, I'm so glad you called. I've been wanting to call you, but I was afraid you'd still be angry. Amy told me everything. About the puppies and the way she and Meg put your name in the hat. If only I'd been there," she said, her words tumbling out in a rush of emotion, "I would have done the same."

"You would?" Cricket couldn't believe what she'd heard.

"Of course!" Brittany said. "So you've got to take the money now. I don't need it. The camera can wait."

For a moment—just for a moment—Cricket was tempted. How easy it would be. Brittany could forget

68

about the camera and all her troubles would be over. But then, what about the club? Would they argue every time about who deserved the money? Would the girl who was pushiest or who had the biggest sob story be the one to get it? "No," she said firmly. "I don't need it, either. I mean, I do, but I want to take my chances at getting it just like everyone else. If we're going to have a club like this, it's the only fair way to do it."

Brittany started to object, but Cricket stopped her. "Besides, you do need the camera," she said. Then, wanting to get it over with once and for all, she went on. "I think you should bring the money to school tomorrow. You can leave it with Ms. Uchida in the office for safekeeping. After school we'll go to the camera shop. You can buy the camera and then you can take pictures of us at Elmer's."

"Do you mean it?" said Brittany. "Are you sure?"

"Yes," said Cricket firmly, speaking as much to herself as to Brittany. "Besides, we're going to be earning lots of money soon. I thought up a project."

"Oh, Cricket, you did? What is it?" Brittany's voice sounded excited now rather than worried. "Tell me."

Cricket quickly described the project. When she had finished, Brittany was more excited than ever. "That's wonderful!" she said. "You know, ever since I moved to Redwood Grove I've noticed how many people have dogs and how many of them are dirty—the dogs, not the people. In Paris—" She stopped. "I mean . . . well, it's not important," she said.

"Yes, it is," said Cricket. "Listen, Brittany, I know that you lived in Paris, and that you take riding lessons and all, but . . . well, it's okay," she said, hoping Brittany would understand what she meant. "You don't have to keep apologizing for who you are. No one should have to do that."

"No, I guess they shouldn't," said Brittany. "That's what Amy told me, too." She took a breath. "All right then," she said. "What I was going to say is that in Paris people got their dogs washed all the time. My mother's best friend had a little white poodle that was washed every week. A dog grooming service came to the apartment in the morning and picked Pierre up in a little red van with a picture of a poodle on the side. Then they returned Pierre in the afternoon all clean, just like the laundry. They always tied ribbons on his ears and—" Her voice suddenly stopped.

"Brittany?" Cricket thought the line had gone dead. "Are you there?"

"Oh . . . oh, yes." Brittany sounded strange. "It's just that . . . well, I just had a terrific idea. You said we're going to do this next Saturday, didn't you?"

"That's right. My parents said we can use our laundry room. We've got a big tub and my dad's going to buy flea soap. We'll have to get together some towels and maybe some hair dryers. But what's your idea?"

Brittany wouldn't tell. "I can't. Not now," she said excitedly. "I have to make sure first. But if we can do it . . . Oh, Cricket, it will be perfect! Just perfect!"

Chapter

I can't believe you're being so mysterious," said Amy. "How could you go the whole day without telling us? It's just too cruel!"

Cricket agreed. It was Monday afternoon, and the four girls were walking from school to downtown Redwood Grove. They were going to stop at the camera shop and then go on to Elmer's.

Brittany had been looking like the cat that swallowed the canary all day. She had the money for the camera tucked away in the pocket of her beige suede jacket—an Adrienne Logan original—and the idea she'd refused to tell Cricket about tucked away in her head. She still wasn't telling.

Meg, who'd arrived at school carrying a mysterious-looking manila envelope, which she'd quickly hidden away in her desk, wasn't either.

"You should at least tell *me*," complained Cricket.

"Both of you. I'm the one who thought up this project. I have to know everything if it's going to be a success."

"You will," said Meg. "But not until we get to Elmer's." She shifted the manila envelope to her left hand so that Cricket, who was walking on her right, couldn't grab it. It wasn't that she was being mean, although she did sort of like keeping everyone guessing. It was just that she hadn't wanted to open the envelope at school. She'd heard about business spies. They were a big problem in computer software companies like the one where her mother worked. Ideas are as valuable as money, Mrs. Kelly had told her. That was why the new programs her company was developing had to be kept absolutely secret. So, suppose someone—a sixth grader perhaps—saw what was in the envelope, then stole their idea and held a dog wash before them? It wasn't worth taking the chance, Meg thought. Though, of course, she was every bit as eager as Cricket and Amy to know what Brittany's secret was.

"I'll tell you at Elmer's, too," Brittany promised. "I want to have the camera first so I can take a picture of your faces when you hear it," she said. "I think we should take pictures of everything we do and put them all in the scrapbook, just like the original club did. Too bad I didn't have the camera on—" She was about to say Saturday, but stopped herself just in time.

Cricket was glad that she did. She and Brittany *had* made things up, though Cricket suspected she might always feel a twinge of jealousy about things like riding lessons. But she didn't want to be reminded of Saturday. Some of the pictures from *that* meeting might not have been so pretty!

"Well, all I can say is I think you're being heartless," said Amy, as they turned a corner and crossed the parking lot next to Harvey's Health Foods, where Meg's grandfather bought his bean sprouts and tofu. The camera shop was located halfway down the block, between a jewelry store and a bank, just across the street from the Redwood Grove Medical Building. A white banner with the word *SALE!* printed on it was hanging in the window. "Tell us your idea now, Brittany," Amy urged as they came to a halt in front of the shop. "Then we can pretend to look surprised for the camera. How about it?"

Brittany wasn't listening. She was staring into the store window, her eyes sparkling with excitement. "There it is," she murmured, pointing to a compact-looking camera displayed in front of a travel poster at the back of the window. "Isn't it beautiful!"

Cricket had never thought of cameras as being beautiful. She'd never thought of anybody longing for one, either. But from the look on Brittany's face, she could see that she wanted that camera every bit as much as some other person—herself, for instance— might want a sweet little golden brown puppy.

"It's on sale, too," Meg pointed out.

That was a difference, Cricket thought. Cameras went on sale, but puppies never did—except maybe the ones at the animal shelter.

"You're right," said Brittany, reading the tag. "Just $69.95."

"Then you'll have money left over," declared Amy. "That means *you* can pay for the ice cream at Elmer's!"

"Oh no, it doesn't," said Cricket. Pushing the thought of dogs from the animal shelter out of her mind, she herded the girls into the shop. She wanted to get this camera buying over with. She didn't want to spend any more time thinking about the money in Brittany's pocket that was soon going to be gone for good. "My dad is paying for the ice cream," she announced. "He gave me enough money for all of us, and for buying flea soap for the dog wash, too."

That put everyone, especially Amy, in a good mood. Brittany, of course, didn't need any extra reason to feel good. She soon had the camera in her hands and was listening intently as the salesclerk explained its features. Cricket was surprised at how much she seemed to know about photography.

"I've gone on a few photo shoots with my mother," Brittany explained. "That's when they take pictures of models wearing the clothes she designed. I always like watching the photographers work, and I've listened to them talk about what they look for in a camera. This one is good for me because it adjusts the focus automatically. I can take a close-up or a distance shot without changing anything."

"Let me see," said Amy. She took the camera from Brittany's hands and aimed it out the door as Brittany paid her money to the clerk. "This is neat!" she exclaimed. "Much better than—Hey, look," she interrupted herself. "There's your mother, Cricket. She's going into that building across the street."

Cricket looked in the direction Amy was pointing, but she didn't see her mother. "Where? What building?" she said.

"That one. The Redwood Grove Medical Building," replied Amy. "She just went inside. I know, let's go show her the camera." Without waiting, she dashed out the door, Brittany's camera in hand.

Cricket wanted to move. But her feet felt like they were nailed to the floor. Why would her mother be going into a medical building? What was in there besides doctors and sick people?

"She's probably just getting a checkup," said Meg quickly. "Come on. We'll find out." She grabbed Cricket by the arm and pulled her out the door after Amy.

"Hey, wait," called Brittany. "My camera." She said a quick "*Merci* . . . I mean, thank you" to the salesclerk, pocketed her change, and dashed out the door after them. By the time she caught up, the girls were inside the medical building studying a list of doctors' offices posted on the wall.

"She must have gone up on the elevator," Amy said. "If we just knew what kind of doctor she was seeing we could find her. But all these specialties have such weird names."

Cricket stared at the list. Amy was right. The specialties printed after each doctor's name seemed to be written in another language. Podiatry, Psychiatry, Ophthalmology, Dermatology, Obstetrics, Orthopedics, Otolaryngology. She could barely read the words, much less figure out what they meant.

"If my dad was here, he could tell us," said Amy. "Since he's a doctor he knows about all this stuff. Oops, sorry about running off with this," she added, handing the camera back to Brittany. She didn't seem to notice the look on Cricket's face. But Meg did.

"Too bad we missed her," she said. "But there's no point in waiting. Doctor's appointments take so long, even if you're in for the tiniest little thing—like a hangnail or something."

Cricket knew Meg was trying to cheer her up. Though she didn't think her mother had a hangnail, she forced herself to smile. "I guess so," she said bravely. "Anyway, we have to get to Elmer's and start planning."

"And eating," said Amy, leading the way out of the medical building. "I don't know about the rest of you, but I'm starved!"

Elmer's Ice Cream Emporium was just a few blocks from the camera store and the medical building, but it could have been a few miles for all Cricket noticed. She couldn't get that list of names out of her mind. So many doctors, so many specialties. And they all sounded serious. It wasn't until they were seated in one of the old-fashioned leather booths at the back of Elmer's, and Brittany had put film in her camera and was ready to take a picture, that she snapped back to the present.

"You see, it has a timer," Brittany was saying, placing the camera on the counter across from the booth where the girls were sitting. "You just set the camera up, press this button, and in thirty seconds it takes the picture." She pressed the button, then slid quickly into place in the booth beside the rest of them. "Now smile," she said as the flash went off.

"That'll be convenient," said Amy, looking impressed. "We can have pictures of all four of us even when there's no one around to take them. Now how about getting down to serious business. I want to know what's in that envelope, Meg! I can't wait a minute longer."

Cricket had almost forgotten about Meg's mysterious envelope. Now, as Meg picked it up and unbent the metal fastener, she almost forgot about her mother going into the medical building. "I can't wait, either," she said. Pushing the thought of doctors further back in her mind, she leaned forward eagerly to see what Meg would pull out.

Meg reached into the envelope and pulled out a bunch of papers. Cricket saw they were covered with pictures and words as Meg spread them out on the table.

"Flyers!" said Cricket. "They're just what we need."

"I made them on the computer," explained Meg proudly. "I did a bunch of different designs so we could have a choice. Once we decide which one we like best, I'll print more copies so we can put them up all over town!"

The flyers Meg had designed to advertise the dog wash were beautiful, and eye-catching, too. Some had pictures of dogs, others had borders of soap suds or balloons. She'd used a variety of type styles and sizes for the words announcing the dog wash on Saturday.

"These are terrific," said Cricket looking through them admiringly.

"They really are," agreed Amy. "Especially this one." She held up a flyer with a picture of a big dog sitting in one corner and a smaller dog in the other. "How did you ever draw such good pictures?"

Meg wished she could claim credit as an artist, but she had to be honest. "Actually, they were pretty simple to make," she admitted. "I used a program from my mom's company that does most of the work for you. It supplies all the pictures and the layouts, and it's easy to make changes, too. See how I didn't fill in the price of the dog wash? Well, I can just go back and add that later when we've decided what to charge."

That's when Brittany, who'd been quietly admiring the flyers, spoke up. "You'll have to add something else, too," she said. "Just one short line. Free pickup and delivery—by limousine!"

"By limousine!" Cricket echoed.

"So that's your idea," said Meg.

"I don't believe it," Amy said. "You mean we can use that big black limousine to pick up dogs?"

"That's right." Brittany was so excited that she forgot about taking pictures. "I thought of it when I was telling Cricket yesterday about how my mother had a friend whose dog was picked up every week to be washed. I remembered that Saturday is the last day we're going to have the limousine, so I asked my parents and Henry, who drives the car, and they agreed. So it's all set! I mean . . . that is . . . if you want it," she added, slipping back for a moment into her old habit of uncertainty.

"Want it? Of course we want it!" exclaimed Cricket. "Limousine service for a bunch of dirty dogs. Redwood Grove may never be the same!"

They spent the next hour eating ice cream—milkshakes for Amy and Brittany, strawberry sundaes for Cricket and Meg—and working out the details. Amy volunteered to bring towels. With a family their size, she said, they had tons of old ones. They'd each bring a hair dryer, and they'd all be responsible for putting up flyers and handing them out wherever and whenever they could. They settled on a design—the one Amy had liked best—and decided on a price.

"I think we should charge five dollars a dog, no matter what size," said Cricket, who'd thought about it in bed last night when she was too excited to sleep. "That way we won't get into arguments about whether a dog qualifies as large or small."

"Good idea," agreed Meg. "And I know just how to say it on the flyer." She borrowed a pencil from the waitress and quickly wrote a few lines. "How's this?"

No dog too large
No dog too small
One price for all!

"Perfect!" said Cricket. And really, it was. In fact, everything they planned seemed perfect—the towels, the hair dryers, the flyers, the price—and, of course, the limousine! It wasn't until later, after Cricket and Meg had said good-bye to Brittany and Amy and were walking together toward home, that Cricket began to have doubts.

"What'll we do if it rains?" she said, glancing nervously at the sky. "The weather looks all right now, but who knows how it will be by Saturday. People won't want to get their dogs washed on a rainy day, will they? Or what if the limousine breaks down and we have to pick up the dogs in my dad's VW bus? We might get sued for false advertising. Maybe our water heater will break again, or we'll run out of flea soap. Or maybe people won't want their dogs washed at all. Maybe we won't get a single customer!"

"You're just getting the jitters," Meg said. "I know

because I do that myself when things seem to be going too well. But I'm sure we'll get plenty of customers. I'll finish the flyers tonight and we can put them up all over town tomorrow. As for flea soap—" She stopped and checked where they were. "Let's go get it right now. You have the money from your dad, and isn't there a pet shop on the next block?"

There was. Meg, who was still new to Redwood Grove, hadn't had a chance to explore it yet, but Cricket knew it almost as well as she knew her own house. The Redwood Grove Pet Shop was easily her favorite store in town. When Pete was alive, she'd gone there all the time to buy his favorite chew sticks. She'd spent hours watching the baby rabbits and kittens playing in the front windows, and talking to the myna birds inside. The birds seemed to recognize her now as she and Meg walked through the door. "Hello, hello," one of them called out in its sing-song voice, tilting its shiny black head in her direction. Its friend on an adjoining perch let out a loud whistle.

"What a great place," said Meg, looking around the crowded store at the tanks full of hamsters and mice, the cages of canaries and finches. "And there are lots of customers. This would be a good place to put up a flyer. Is there a bulletin board?"

"Yes, over there by the kitty litter," replied Cricket. "I'll show you." She was as familiar with the bulletin board as she was with the myna birds and the chew stick display. The owner of the shop let everyone put up notices as long as they related to pets. It was there that she'd first learned about the Sunny Hill Kennels. She saw now, with a sinking feeling in her stomach, that Mrs. Wilson had already put up a card announcing the birth of Cindy's puppies. "Ten golden beauties," it said. "Excellent pet and show stock. Reserve yours now."

Meg glanced at the card, too, but her attention was quickly caught by another sheet of paper tacked to the board. "This is interesting," she said. "Here's a list of prices from a professional dog groomer. Comfort clips, $50. Plain baths, $15-$20. Flea baths, $20-$25. That's a lot!"

"It certainly is!"

Cricket and Meg turned to see a tiny gray-haired lady studying the bulletin board with them.

"Much more than I can afford," she said.

"Really?" Cricket felt a shiver of excitement travel down her spine. Could this be a customer? "Do you have a dog?" she asked eagerly.

"Yes, indeed," the lady replied. "His name's Buster. He's a dear, but he does get dirty and bathing him has gotten to be a bit much for me lately. But these prices . . ." She shook her head and clicked her tongue disapprovingly.

Cricket and Meg exchanged a glance. Meg immediately reached into the manila envelope she was carrying and pulled out one of her sample flyers. "Maybe we can help," she said, handing the flyer to the lady.

"We're having a dog wash this Saturday."

"There are four of us," Cricket added. "We have a club called Always Friends. We'll do an excellent job and we're only charging five dollars."

"Well, isn't that something," the woman said, studying the flyer. "Very enterprising. Reminds me of my own youth. I was always starting businesses—baking cookies, baby-sitting, even walking dogs." She paused to look at the address. "Why, this isn't too far from my house," she said. "Buster and I could walk right over." She smiled at the girls. "You've got a deal," she said, putting the flyer in her purse and heading out the door. "See you on Saturday!"

Cricket's worries flew right out the door with the woman. "We did it!" she exclaimed, giving Meg a high five. "Our very first customer. We're on our way!"

Chapter

Meg's flyers went up the next day. The girls tacked them to telephone poles and bulletin boards all over town. Amy got the idea of sticking them under the windshield wipers of parked cars, especially those that had dogs inside. And Cricket took a stack to Dr. Harding, the veterinarian who'd treated Pete. She hadn't been in his office since Pete had died, and stepping through the door brought back a flood of bittersweet memories.

"Could I leave some of these in your waiting room?" she asked, showing him the flyers as she fought back the lump that had risen in her throat.

"Why, of course, Cricket," he said. "This looks like a good idea. I'm sure you'll pick up some customers here. And how about you?" he asked, smiling kindly over the glasses he always wore perched on the tip of his nose. "Have you thought about getting another dog? Any dog would be lucky to have an owner like you."

"I'm working on it," said Cricket. She didn't want to tell him about Cindy's puppies. She didn't plan to visit the kennel, or even think about them if she could help it, until the dog wash was over. She had a superstitious feeling that seeing the puppies might jinx things.

There was one place she couldn't avoid visiting, though—the animal shelter. She was tricked into it when her father asked her to drive to the print shop with him on Wednesday after school. He had to pick up copies of a literary magazine his students at Redwood Grove High School were putting out. "You can make some more copies of your flyers there," he said. "It looks like your supply is getting low. And we can pick up a pizza on the way home. Your mom doesn't feel much like cooking."

Cricket didn't like the sound of that. When had her mother ever *not* felt like cooking? Even when she'd spent all day filling orders, she always liked making dinner for her family. "It's relaxing for me. No pressure—just cooking for the people I love," she always said. But now . . .

Cricket hadn't mentioned seeing her mother going into the medical building. She didn't want her to think she was spying. Besides, what if she did bring up the subject, and her mother broke down and told her that something awful was happening. Awful things *did* happen, Cricket knew. Look at Meg. Her father had died when she was little. Cricket didn't think she could bear anything like that.

Though she tried not to think about it, she couldn't shake the creepy feeling that came over her until they had finished at the copy shop and were back in the car. Mr. Connors glanced at her out of the corner of his eye. "You know what, Cricket?" he said, suddenly sounding unusually hearty. "I just realized this road goes right past the animal shelter. You've got all those flyers. Why not stop and put one up?"

"But Dad . . ." Cricket started to object, but her father was already turning into the parking lot beside a gray-and-white cinder block building. DRAKE COUNTY ANIMAL SHELTER said the sign over the entranceway. He pulled the car to a stop and turned off the engine.

Cricket knew there was no way out of it, but she wasn't going to let her father get away with thinking she didn't see through him. "Some performance, Dad," she said, climbing out of the car with the flyers. "Academy award-winning material."

"Performance? What performance?" said Mr. Connors innocently. "This is a good place for your flyers. Come on."

A chorus of barking greeted Cricket's ears as she followed her father into the building. In spite of herself, she felt a twinge of excitement at the sound. Being anywhere near a bunch of dogs always did that to her.

"Sure you can put one up," said the woman at the front desk, when Cricket showed her the flyers. "Our bulletin board's over there." She pointed to the wall next to a door marked KENNELS. "And why don't you go back and take a look at the dogs while you're here. We have some really nice ones and they all need good homes."

"Well, maybe just a quick look," Cricket said, her curiosity getting the better of her. She tacked up the notice, then stepped through the door her father held open. The barking reached a crescendo as the dogs in the kennel area rushed up and down the runs, wagging their tails and jumping against the gates, eager to greet whoever had come to see them.

The woman at the desk was right, Cricket thought. There really are some nice dogs here. Forgetting how she'd resisted coming, she reached through the wire to scratch the head of a mournful-eyed basset hound. She laughed at the way a little dog that looked like a dust mop ran around in circles so fast that she couldn't tell its head from its tail. And her heart went out to an old gray-muzzled dog that held out its paw to her hopefully.

There were red and blue cards attached to all the runs. "What do the different colors mean?" Mr. Connors asked a young man who was sweeping the aisle between the kennels.

The man stopped sweeping and smiled as if he were truly glad to see them. "The red ones are for dogs we just got in," he said. "We keep them for two weeks to give their owners a chance to claim them. Like this guy." He grinned at a big Irish setter that seemed to grin back at him, its tongue lolling out of its mouth. "He's a regular with us. He's always taking off and then forgetting how to get home. His owners will probably be in today to pick him up. The dogs that aren't claimed get a blue tag. That means they're available for adoption. We keep them for another two weeks to see if anyone wants them. We've got some great dogs," he said eagerly. "Are you here to adopt?"

"No," replied Cricket quickly, not looking at her father—nor at the basset hound with the mournful eyes. "But what happens after the second two weeks?" she asked. Even as she asked it, she realized what the answer would be.

The young man's face told the whole story. "We can't afford to keep them all," he said, looking pained, as if he didn't want to think about what happened. "We're able to find homes for most of them, but then . . . well . . . we do it as humanely as possible," he said.

"You mean you kill them." Cricket turned away. The old dog with the gray muzzle looked up at her.

"We put them to sleep," said the young man. But his choice of words didn't make it any better. Neither did her father's apology in the car.

"I'm sorry, Cricket. I didn't mean to upset you," he said. "They really do find homes for most of the dogs. For those that they don't . . . well, you can't save the whole world, can you?"

"But you can try," said Cricket. "Maybe if we earn enough money from the dog wash, we can give the shelter a donation so they can afford to hold the dogs longer. That would at least save a few."

"Yes, it probably would," said Mr. Connors. "That would be a very generous thing for your club to do." He looked at his daughter proudly. "And as for those puppies at the Sunny Hill Kennels, your mother and I will try to help somehow. We've got a lot of expenses right now and we may have more in the future, but . . . Anyway, you're certainly doing your part. I can't wait to see how the dog wash turns out."

Neither could Cricket. And now she had an added incentive for making it a success.

"I think that's a wonderful idea," said Meg when Cricket phoned her later, after she and her dad had eaten the pizza and her mother, who'd barely swallowed three bites, had once again shuffled off to bed. "Maybe we should make that one of the goals of the club—donating extra money to good causes, like the shelter. I'm sure Brittany and Amy will agree. And I'll bet we will have money left over from the dog wash. We've already had calls from twelve people for limousine pickup, and there are bound to be more customers who'll just show up at the door—like that lady we met at the pet shop. Oh, this is going to be so much fun!" she exclaimed. "And listen, Cricket . . ." She hesitated for a moment, as if she wasn't sure she should say what she was going to say. "I wouldn't worry too much about your mother."

"What do you mean?" Cricket felt suddenly alert. "Do you know something?"

"Not exactly. But I think my mom does," replied Meg. "And from the way she's been acting, I'd say it's not anything too bad. I think Amy's doing some investigating, too," she added.

"Amy? But—"

"Look, let's not talk about it now," said Meg, cutting her off. "I probably shouldn't have mentioned it. You've got enough to think about just getting ready for Saturday, and now I'm getting nervous, too. I just hope the limousine doesn't break down. I hope we have enough towels. And I hope it doesn't rain!"

It didn't.

The moment Cricket woke up on Saturday morning, she knew it was going to be a beautiful day. Sunlight was streaming in through her window, and when she jumped out of bed, she realized it was warm enough for shorts and an old paint-splattered T-shirt—perfect dog-washing clothes. She brushed her teeth and ran a comb through her hair, and headed into the kitchen where her father was cracking eggs into a sizzling pan of bacon grease. Her mother was sitting on the deck outside the French doors that led to the backyard, sipping a cup of herb tea. She looked sort of pale, but she was smiling to herself, as if she had some kind of secret.

"What an absolutely perfect day," she said when

she saw Cricket. "The dogs can run around in the yard to dry off and—" She moved farther away from the doors as the smell of frying eggs drifted out of the house. Her face turned a bit paler beneath her freckles.

"Mom," Cricket began. She hadn't said anything all week, but now she had to know. "Are you really all right? Meg said—"

But just then the bell outside the kitchen door rang.

"It's Meg," Mr. Connors called. And in a second Meg herself, dressed in shorts and an old T-shirt like Cricket's, burst through the door and out onto the deck. "It's D-day!" she said. "*D* as in dog. Is the laundry room ready? The water heater working? Have we got enough soap? How about the dog biscuits?" They were planning on giving dog biscuits for treats. "And where in the world is Brittany and that limousine?"

Mrs. Connors laughed. "I can see that you girls had better get busy. That's what I always do when I get nervous. Just plunge right into work and the jitters go away." She stood up and poured the rest of her herb tea over the rose bushes. She insisted it was what made them bloom so beautifully.

"Anyone want some eggs?" called Mr. Connors. "You're going to need lots of energy today. Oh, wait." He looked out the kitchen window. "There's the limousine," he announced. "Boy, I never thought I'd see the day when a car like that was parked in our driveway."

Forgetting about the eggs, as well as about asking

her mother questions, Cricket rushed out the kitchen door with Meg at her heels. Brittany, wearing shorts and a T-shirt like the other girls but still managing to look like she'd stepped out of the pages of a fashion magazine, was getting out of the car. Henry, the driver, wearing his blue uniform and a big friendly smile, held the door open for her.

"Are we going to have fun today, or what?" he said, grinning at the girls. "I've chauffeured all kinds—businesspeople, authors, even some rock stars—but never a bunch of dogs. Though come to think of it, that's how some of the people have acted."

"Well, these dogs are going to be very well behaved. At least, I hope so," said Brittany, glancing nervously at the pale gray upholstery that lined the car's spacious interior. "Where's Amy?" she asked. "She's supposed to do the first round of pickups with us. We've got to start soon."

"Oh, don't worry. She'll be here," said Meg, climbing into the back of the limousine and pretending she was a rock star. Brittany whipped out her camera and took a picture of her. "She's not going to miss taking another ride in this."

"I'd sort of like to know where we're going," said Henry. "Do you have the addresses? I may have to look at a map."

"I'll get the list for you," said Cricket. As she headed back into the house, she was suddenly overcome by a case of nerves. Suppose Henry couldn't find the dogs they were supposed to pick up? She'd written down the names and addresses—fifteen in all—but she hadn't thought to ask for directions. And how about a map? Did Henry have one in the car? Would he be able to figure out where all the twisty roads in Redwood Grove led? Would he be able to get the long black car up them?

She hurried into the living room, picked up the list from the table by the phone, and was heading back to the kitchen when the front doorbell rang. Amy, she thought. At least that's one less thing to worry about. If she hadn't shown up . . .

She opened the door and was almost knocked off her feet as a pony-sized mass of white fur, straining at the end of a leash held by a breathless little gray-haired lady, jumped up on her.

"Buster, down!" commanded the lady—the same lady that she and Meg had met in the pet shop. "Behave yourself now."

Buster paid no attention. Wiggling all over with excitement, he planted his front feet on Cricket's shoulders and eagerly licked her face. Cricket staggered slightly, wiped her face, and noticed that Buster had the biggest, darkest, most beautiful dog eyes she'd ever seen.

"Looks like he likes you," said the lady, catching her breath. "He always likes young people. I'm afraid it's a bit hard for him living with an old bird like me." She tugged again at Buster's leash. This time he paid attention and sat down politely. But he kept his eyes fixed on Cricket.

"Well, I like him, too," Cricket said, recovering herself. And she did. In fact, something about Buster seemed awfully familiar. She had the same kind of feeling she'd had when she first met Meg—as if there were some sort of connection between them. She laughed as Buster cocked his head, listening as if he understood every word she said. His shaggy, rather dirty, fur was completely white, except for a brown patch over one ear. It stood out in tufts over his eyes and drooped gracefully over his muzzle, making him look like a doggy version of Albert Einstein, the famous scientist, whose picture hung on the wall in Cricket's classroom at school. "He's not quite what I expected," she said. "Somehow, I thought he'd be . . . well . . ."

"Smaller?" suggested the lady. "I can see why you might have thought that. To tell you the truth, Buster is not exactly the dog I would have chosen for myself. As it was, he chose me. He showed up at my house one day, lost. I tried to find his owners, but I couldn't, so I took him in. Sometimes I'm afraid he'll be the end of me. You can see why I have a hard time bathing him."

Cricket certainly could. In fact, she wondered how they would manage themselves. But she took Buster's leash from the lady and said confidently, "Don't worry, we'll do a good job. You can pick him up this afternoon. Oh, there's Amy," she interrupted herself, as a car driven by one of Amy's brothers pulled up at the curb. Amy leaped out. A black-and-white mop of a dog with a pushed-in face and round black eyes was in her arms. Instead of heading straight for the limousine parked in the driveway, as Cricket expected her to do, she hurried up the walk to the house.

"Well, I'd better be going," said Buster's owner. She descended the front steps carefully. "Have to watch out for falls at my age," she explained with a smile. Then she hurried off down the walk.

Cricket suddenly realized she hadn't gotten her name. Before she could call out to her, though, Amy charged up the steps.

"My neighbor's," she said, setting the little black-and-white dog down. Buster wagged his tail enthusiastically and sniffed at the dog like a vacuum cleaner. "It's a shih tzu," said Amy. "From Tibet or somewhere."

"Well, it looks like it'll be easier to wash than this guy," said Cricket, patting Buster's head fondly. "I'm glad you got here, Amy. We were all getting a little nervous. Anyway, here's the list of dogs you and Brittany are picking up." She handed the paper to Amy. "You'd better get going."

Amy took the paper but she didn't dash away to the limousine. Instead, she pulled Cricket and the dogs into the house. "I've got something to show you," she said. "It's about your mom."

"My mom?" Cricket suddenly felt cold. Buster

whimpered and pushed his nose against her hand. It was exactly what Pete used to do when he sensed she was upset.

"Yes," said Amy. "Meg told me you were worried about her being sick or something, so I decided to go back to the medical building and write down the names of all the specialties on that list. Then last night I got my dad to translate them for me, and—" She pulled a sheet of paper from her pocket.

"What is it?" Cricket said, barely trusting herself to speak. "What does she have? Tell me!"

"I don't know for sure," said Amy, holding out the paper. "But the way it looks to me, either she's crazy or she's having a baby!"

Chapter

9

A baby?" Cricket grabbed the paper from Amy's hands. The list of doctors' specialties was print-ed out in a column, followed by Amy's notes about what they did. Suddenly all those weird-sounding words made sense. Podiatry had something to do with feet, ophthalmology with eyes, orthopedics with bones, otolaryngology with the throat, dermatology with skin, psychiatry with mental problems, and obstetrics with having babies!

"I don't know if she has any mental problems," said Amy. "But from what Meg told me there's nothing wrong with her feet or her eyes."

"Not with her bones, or her throat, or her skin, either," said Cricket, still feeling dazed. "At least I don't think so. But a baby . . ." She could hardly believe it.

"Cricket?" Mrs. Connors called. "What's taking

you so long?" She came into the living room from the kitchen and was almost knocked off her feet, just as Cricket had been, by Buster. "Whoa," she cried, staggering back as he placed his paws on her shoulders and licked her face. "Who's this?"

"His name's Buster," replied Cricket automatically. "He belongs to a lady we met in the pet shop. And this little black-and-white one is a shih tzu that—" But what was she doing, chatting about dogs? Her mother was having a baby! Or was she? "Mom," she said, feeling as if she'd burst if she didn't know the truth right now. "You've got to tell me—are you crazy, or are you having a baby?"

Mrs. Connors's eyes opened wide. She untangled herself from Buster and stared at Cricket and Amy in astonishment. "You girls," she said. "How did you find out?"

"Then it's true?" said Cricket. "Tell me—yes or no?"

"Yes," replied her mother, breaking out in a smile. "Yes, it's true!"

"Oh, I've got to tell Meg and Brittany!" Amy exclaimed. "They're going to be so excited. And to think that I'm the one who figured it out!" She grabbed the little shih tzu, who'd been watching in bewilderment, and raced out the door.

Cricket didn't know what to say. The truth was just beginning to sink in. Her mother was all right. She wasn't sick. "Oh, Mom," she cried, flinging her arms around her. "I've been so worried. I was afraid you were going to . . . to end up like Pete."

Mrs. Connors hugged her tight. "I'm sorry you were so worried, Cricket," she said, as Buster tried to nose his way in between them, just as Pete had always done when hugs didn't include him. "Your dad and I were planning to tell you tomorrow, after all the excitement of the dog wash was over. I didn't realize you had a detective working on it."

"That was Amy's idea," said Cricket. "I didn't have anything to do with it. She saw you going into the medical building when we were downtown Monday. Meg told her I was worried about you, so she asked her dad what all those doctors specialize in. Then she—or I guess by then it was we—put two and two together."

"Well, you girls are more clever than I was," Mrs. Connors said, laughing now. Buster, deciding things were all right, flopped down on the floor with his head on his paws, looking up at them from beneath his bushy Albert Einstein eyebrows. "I didn't even suspect I might be pregnant until that afternoon when we were talking in the kitchen, after the disaster with the tarts. When I talked to Meg's mother, she suspected it, too. I went to the doctor and got the test results just the other day. The baby will be born in the spring. I'll start feeling better soon, too. Sleepiness and strange tastes in food are pretty common in the first months and—Oh, Cricket," she broke off, "I hope that you're happy about it. Your dad and I have been wanting to have another baby for years, but we'd just about given up hope. We want so much for it to be all right with you, too."

"All right? Mom, of course, it's all right!" exclaimed Cricket. "It's wonderful! The best news I've ever heard. It's a lot better to be having a baby than to be crazy or dead!"

"Well, that's some recommendation for parenthood," said her father, coming into the living room. Buster leaped up from the floor, but he didn't jump on Mr. Connors. Something must have told him that wouldn't go over too well. Instead he sniffed at him politely, then sat down and held out his paw. Cricket's father laughed as he knelt down and shook it. "So the secret's out," he said, giving Cricket a squeeze. "Your pals are all celebrating out there. But I'm afraid if you don't get this dog wash started soon, you're going to have a lot of angry customers."

Of course, he was right. But Cricket couldn't come down to earth so quickly. She practically floated out of the living room with Buster at her heels. A baby, just imagine! Would it be a boy or a girl? Would it have red hair like hers, or brown hair like her dad's? What would they name it? Where would it sleep? And how about dogs? Would it like dogs? It had to like dogs!

Meg and Brittany and Amy were almost as excited as Cricket. The minute she came out the door, Brittany started snapping pictures of her. "So you can see how you looked when you found out," she said. Meg's eyes filled with tears as they always did when she was really, truly happy. "Oh, I hope it's a girl," she sighed. "You can dress her in the sweetest little dresses."

"*If* she likes dresses," put in Amy. "Not all girls do, you know, and she might even be a boy! At least you'll get to be a big sister," she said enviously. "I'm afraid I'm doomed to spend the rest of my life as a *little* sister."

"Well, I'm afraid you girls are going to be out of business if we don't get going," said Henry, getting back into the car and starting the engine. "Save the baby talk for later. Now it's time to think about dogs."

"That's right," agreed Cricket. "We'd better check the laundry room, Meg, and make sure we're ready to start washing."

"You can practice on Rambo here," Amy said, thrusting the little black-and-white dust mop into Cricket's arms. She climbed into the limousine after Brittany and gave the list of addresses to Henry. "We'll bring back as many dogs as we can on this trip, and then go back and pick up the rest."

Rambo—if that was really his name or just Amy's idea of a joke—whimpered as the limousine pulled out of the driveway. "Don't worry, she'll be back," Cricket assured him. "Now it's bath time for you. And you, too, Buster," she added as the big white dog pranced around her and Rambo jealously. "Come on."

The laundry room, where Cricket and Meg and their first furry customers headed, had two large laundry sinks attached to the wall and a big metal tub set up on the cement floor. Cricket's father had screwed a hose with a spray attachment to one of the faucets. The floor had a drain in the center, so they'd be able to lift the dogs out of the tubs and rinse them off there with the hose. Neat piles of dry towels, plus supplies of flea soap and dog shampoo, were stacked on the counter above the Connors's washer and dryer.

Brittany, who was good with numbers, had figured out exactly how long they should spend washing each dog. She'd worked it all out on paper, dividing the number of minutes in the day by the number of dogs they had to wash. Then she'd made up a chart and taped it to the wall. It was very impressive. Orderly, too, with time out for lunch and an afternoon snack break.

Cricket felt hungry already. She wished she'd taken her dad up on his offer of eggs. "Let's wash the little dog first. He'll be easier to do," she said, pushing the thought of food *and* the new baby out of her mind. If she thought about babies now, she'd never be able to concentrate on all the work they had to do.

Meg started filling one of the washtubs with water.

Cricket led Buster out to the backyard. "Now be a good dog," she said, patting him on the back. Buster cocked his head inquiringly, as if wondering what she meant.

When Cricket returned to the laundry room, Meg was already lowering Rambo into the tub. Luckily, he didn't live up to his name. He stood in the warm water, his front paws on the rim of the tub, gazing at them reproachfully as they shampooed his fur and then rinsed him off.

"Well, that was easy," Cricket declared, toweling the little dog off. "Now, let's do Buster. We'll have plenty of time to finish with him before Amy and Brittany get back with the others." She left Meg to dry Rambo with one of the blow dryers and went out to the yard.

"Buster," she called. She didn't see him anywhere. Had he gotten out? But how could he? She'd inspected the entire fence yesterday to make sure there were no loose boards or holes. "Buster!" she called again, getting worried. She put her lips together and whistled, and all at once what looked like a dirt-colored polar bear leaped up from Mrs. Connors's flower bed.

"Oh, no! Buster, how could you!" Cricket exclaimed, staring at the huge hole he'd dug among the chrysanthemums. "You're a bad dog," she said, making a dive for his collar. Buster dodged out of reach. He stretched his front paws in front of him, tongue lolling out of his mouth, ready for fun. Then he leaped up and raced around the yard with Cricket after him. "Buster, stop!" she shouted as he bounded up onto the deck, through the French doors, and into the living room.

He leaped straight up on the sofa with his dirty feet. "No!" cried Cricket, lunging for him. This time she got hold of his collar.

"What's going on in there?" her father called from the dining room, where he and her mother were discussing whether they could afford to add a room to the house for the new baby.

"Nothing, Dad," Cricket replied quickly. She brushed off the sofa as best she could and dragged Buster back to the laundry room. "You are trouble!" she said. "If you were my dog I'd take you to obedience school. You're too big to dig holes in the garden and jump on the sofa."

Buster, who'd been hanging his head contritely, wagged his tail and whimpered as if he agreed.

"You know what I think?" said Meg, as they rinsed the dirt off his thick white coat and then heaved him into the big metal tub on the floor. "I think Buster's the dog of your dreams."

"The dog of my dreams?" Cricket looked at the mountain of wet white fur and soapsuds looming in front of her. How could Meg possibly say that? Buster was about as far from a sweet little golden-colored puppy as you could get. Then suddenly, she realized what Meg meant. Buster was literally the dog of her dreams. "You're right!" she said. "Now I know why he seemed so familiar. Except for that brown ear, he looks and acts exactly like the dog I dreamed about."

"Well, I just hope no more dream dogs show up," said Meg, "or we really will run out of shampoo!"

They rinsed Buster off with the hose, and after he'd given himself a shake that left both of them dripping, they dried him off as well as they could. It took nearly the whole stack of clean towels. "He's too big for blow drying," Cricket said. "It would take hours. I'll make a bed for him in the garage. It's warm in there. He'll dry off and he'll stay out of mischief until his owner comes to get him."

Buster seemed happy enough to settle down in the garage. He flopped onto the old blanket Cricket spread out for him, chewing contentedly on a giant-sized dog biscuit. He didn't deserve a reward, of course, but when he turned those big brown eyes on Cricket, she couldn't resist. Rambo, lying in the sun on the deck, was already munching on his fifth miniature-sized biscuit.

"How about a reward for us now?" said Cricket. She opened the bread box in the kitchen and took out a couple of bagels, tossed one to Meg and kept one for herself. "Here's to babies and dream dogs, and . . . well, just about everything!" she said. Her stomach growled hungrily and she gobbled up the bagel as if it were the last food she'd ever see.

It very nearly was. Because as soon as Amy and Brittany returned with the first carload of dogs, everything civilized and orderly—Brittany's carefully drawn up schedule, the plans for lunch and afternoon snacks—went right out the window. It was soon apparent that if they were going to finish anytime before next week, everyone would have to wash dogs. Cricket's father set up an extra tub on the deck and her mother—after assuring Cricket that she was up to it and that it wouldn't hurt her and certainly wouldn't hurt the baby—started washing dogs in the bathtub. Cricket threw one damp towel after another into the clothes dryer and Amy ran the hair dryers full blast.

All through the afternoon, a steady stream of people who'd seen the flyers around town appeared at the door with their dirty dogs. Fortunately, none was as large as Buster, and only a few got into fights. Just one—a sulky, low-slung dachshund and cocker mix—turned out to be a digger like Buster and had to be dragged repeatedly out of the flower beds.

Brittany ran around taking pictures of everything—dogs that were dirty and then clean, people who were dry and then wet. By late afternoon, when Henry was ready to drive the last group of clean dogs home, her hair was tangled and her T-shirt was grimy, but her face was glowing happily. For the first time since Cricket had met her, she did not look like she'd stepped out of a fashion magazine. "I can't wait to develop this film," she said, taking one last picture of the carload of dogs. "We're going to fill pages and pages in the scrapbook."

"Well, I can't wait to count the money," said Amy, pushing a strand of wet black hair out of her eyes. "So many people brought dogs to the door, I lost track of how much we were making."

"So did I," said Cricket, who'd been in charge of collecting the money. "But it's all in the cookie tin in the kitchen, except for what the owners of this last bunch of dogs have to pay, and what's owed by a couple of kids who promised to bring their money later. We can go in and count it, but we'll have to wait until my dad's done mopping the floor." She didn't want to think about what her mother was dealing with, scooping up dog messes in the backyard. Maybe it was good practice though—the new baby would need plenty of dirty diapers changed!

"I'm too tired to count anything now," groaned Meg. "I'm sure we've got more than one hundred dollars, which means we'll be able to give a good donation to the animal shelter. Why don't we just all come back here tomorrow and pick who gets to spend the money. If you get chosen, Cricket, I want to go to the kennels with you," she added. "I'm dying to see those puppies."

Cricket still didn't want to jinx things by thinking about Cindy's puppies. She was *not* going to get her hopes up. She was not going to be hurt again. "Sure," she said quickly. "But I'm not counting on anything this time." She cast a guilty glance at Brittany. She still felt bad about the way she'd behaved last Saturday, and she wanted to be sure that this time they played by the rules. "Don't forget, it's got to be a fair drawing," she said. "Everyone puts her name in."

"Except me," said Brittany, climbing into the car along with Amy and the dogs. She had her camera in her hands. "I've already had my chance. But I'm going to keep my fingers crossed for you, Cricket."

"Me, too," Meg said, climbing in after her. Though her grandparents' house was only a short distance away, she was just too exhausted to walk.

"And me," Amy piped up. "Even though I am jealous of you for getting to be a big sister!"

"I guess I'll keep my fingers crossed, too," said Henry with a grin. "Might as well make it unanimous. Good luck, kid," he called, as he backed the limousine out of the drive.

Cricket watched the long black car disappear down the block. Every bone in her body seemed to ache from lifting sopping wet dogs out of tubs. At the same time, she'd never felt so good. And in a way, though she was glad they'd earned so much, she didn't really care about the money. Just having done a good job seemed enough.

"Well, you did it!" said her father, coming out of the kitchen door, scrub mop in hand. "I had my doubts for awhile," he said, giving her a squeeze, "but you girls managed to get them all washed—even that big white mop of a dog. I'll bet *his* owner was happy."

For a second—just for a second—Cricket didn't know what he was talking about. Then she realized who he meant. "Buster!" she exclaimed. "Oh, no! I forgot all about him!"

She raced to the garage and opened the door. Buster leaped up from the blanket, where he'd been gnawing on something that looked suspiciously like her father's tennis racket, and flung himself at her, wriggling all over and whimpering with joy. "Oh, Buster, I'm so sorry," Cricket said, throwing her arms around him. He smelled clean and felt big and warm and solid, just as Pete had felt.

"Well, he doesn't seem any the worse for wear," said Mr. Connors, patting the gleeful dog on the head. Fortunately, he didn't look into the garage to see what had happened to his tennis racket. "But where's his owner? It's nearly six o'clock. Maybe you should give her a call."

"I guess I'd better," agreed Cricket. "Though I kind of hate to see him go. He's a troublemaker, but there's something about him . . ." She headed into the house with Buster close behind her, looking as if he wasn't planning to let her out of his sight ever again. The yellow pad where Cricket had been writing the names and phone numbers of their customers was on the kitchen counter next to the cookie tin full of money. She picked it up. Buster had been the first dog to arrive, so his owner's name should be—

Then suddenly she remembered. She hadn't gotten the little gray-haired lady's name—not this morning, when she hurried down the walk just as Amy arrived, nor at the pet shop the other day. She had absolutely no idea who she was!

Quickly, she checked Buster's collar for a name tag. She found a metal tag with his license number etched on it, but no name and address. The collar itself looked brand-new. Maybe the woman had bought it at

109

the pet shop. Maybe she'd ordered an address tag, too, but that wasn't any help now.

"Don't worry. She'll probably show up soon," said Mr. Connors when Cricket told him what had happened. "For now, you can feed him some of Pete's kibble. There's still a full bag in the pantry. And I'm going to go get some steaks to throw on the barbecue. Your mom's getting her appetite back—probably from washing all those dogs. I'll pick up some Super Mocha Crunch from Elmer's, and some of their special chocolate fudge sauce, too. We've all got some celebrating to do!"

Cricket wasn't sure whether they were celebrating the arrival of the baby—several months ahead of time—or the departure of a house full of dogs. It didn't matter. She was happy about both, and she was especially happy not to have to worry about her mother anymore.

"Thanks for pitching in today, Mom," she said that night after dinner, as they sat out on the deck finishing their ice cream and watching the stars come out. "I don't think the four of us could have handled all those dogs without help from you and Dad."

"I'd say you were almost too successful," laughed Mrs. Connors. "But what I want to know now is what we're going to do about this guy?" She reached over to pat Buster, who was stretched out on the deck beside them, head on his paws, waiting patiently to be offered some Super Mocha Crunch.

"I don't know," said Cricket. She set her nearly empty ice cream bowl down on the deck for Buster to clean with a few quick licks. "I can't imagine what happened to the lady who owns him. I suppose she might have forgotten she brought him here. She seemed pretty old and old people are forgetful, aren't they?"

"Sometimes," said Mr. Connors. "But Buster's a pretty big thing to forget. I think something must have happened to prevent her from coming. I guess he'll have to spend the night here. Then, if she doesn't show up in the morning, we can take him to the county animal shelter."

"The shelter?" Cricket echoed, looking at her father in alarm.

"Just to help us find the owner," he explained. "Buster has a license. That means they must have some kind of record of him. They can probably look it up and tell us who owns him."

"Oh," said Cricket, feeling relieved. She'd been thinking of those blue tags and what happened at the end of two weeks. "I guess that's all right then," she said. Though when she remembered the sad-eyed basset hound and the old gray-muzzled dog who'd offered her his paw, she really didn't want Buster going anywhere near the animal shelter.

"I suppose that's the best we can do," said her mother, standing up and yawning sleepily. "We'll just hope the owner shows up in the morning. Meanwhile,

I'll make Buster a nice comfy bed in the laundry room. He should be happy in there."

But he wasn't. The house was dark, everyone was asleep, and the dial on Cricket's Betty Boop clock read one-forty when the howling began. At first, Cricket thought it was the siren from the fire station down-town. Then she thought it was a police car. And then, opening her eyes and sitting up in bed, she realized it was Buster. She threw on her bathrobe and hurried out through the living room and into the kitchen. It wouldn't do to have her parents wake up and banish him to the garage. He'd spent enough time out there already.

She opened the door to the laundry room. "Buster," she whispered, bracing herself. She expected him to hurl himself at her as he'd done before. Instead he crawled toward her, whimpering pitifully, and looking like an animated polar bear rug. "Oh, Buster! Don't look like that," she said. "Nobody's punishing you." That was all he needed to hear. In a second, he was wagging his tail. In another second, he was rolling over on his back so that Cricket could scratch his pink and white stomach.

"Silly old dog," she murmured fondly. "Come on. You can sleep on the rug in my room, just like Pete did. But no more howling. Promise?"

Chapter

10

Cricket was having the most incredible dream. She was in the mountains, surrounded by enormous white drifts of snow. But the drifts weren't cold, as snow usually was. They were warm and soft and furry and—Suddenly she woke up.

"Buster!" she exclaimed. The big white dog lying on her bed licked her face and then rolled over, taking most of her comforter with him. "Who said you could come up here?"

Buster, who obviously didn't see why a dog should sleep on the floor when a nice soft bed was available, sighed and gazed at her adoringly with his big dark eyes.

"Cricket, is that dog in there with you?" her mother called. "Because he's not in the laundry room. I hope he didn't get out somehow and run away."

Buster put Mrs. Connors's fears to rest by bounding off the bed, shoving his nose through a crack in the door to open it, and dashing out to the kitchen. Cricket pulled on her robe and stumbled after him. She reached the kitchen just in time to see her mother offering Buster a pumpernickel bagel.

"He sort of grows on you, doesn't he?" Mrs. Connors said sheepishly, as Buster grabbed the bagel. Instead of eating it right away, though, he tossed it into the air with a flip of his nose, leaped up and caught it, then swallowed it in two swift gulps.

"Neat trick!" said Cricket admiringly. "He must be part seal, as well as part polar bear. I'll bet he'd be good with a Frisbee, too. Is Pete's old one still around?"

"I think it's in the pantry near the bag of kibble," replied Mrs. Connors, turning on the coffeepot. "Be careful you don't get too attached to that dog, though," she warned. "Remember, we're going to find his owner, one way or another."

"I know, Mom," said Cricket. "Anyway I don't want a big goofy dog like—" She stopped, suddenly aware that Buster was eyeing her intently. His one brown ear was flipped back over his head, and she had a feeling he'd understood every word that she'd said. "Sorry, Buster. I didn't mean to call you goofy," she apologized. "You're probably really smart. I know, let's try something."

Buster looked at her alertly.

She stood up in front of him, her curly red hair still

tousled from sleep, and tried to look as if she were in charge. "All right, Buster. Sit!" she commanded.

Buster sat.

Cricket wasn't sure if it was her command that did it, or the fact that he had to scratch his ear. But she praised him anyway. "Good boy," she said encouragingly, trying to sound like the dog training lady she'd watched on TV. "Now, lie down!" She didn't really expect him to obey this time, but after a moment's hesitation, he did.

Cricket was amazed. "Did you see that, Mom?" she said.

Buster kept his eyes glued on her, as if waiting for her next order—or maybe for another bagel.

"Someone must have trained him," Cricket said. "I don't think it could have been that lady who brought him here. She didn't seem to have much control over him at all. But maybe whoever owned him before took him to obedience classes. He's probably sort of rusty," she said, remembering the way she'd had to chase him around the yard yesterday. "But I'll bet it would all come back to him pretty quickly."

Whoever had trained Buster to sit and lie down must have played Frisbee with him, too. After breakfast, when Cricket and her father took him out to the backyard, he turned out to be a champion player, leaping and catching the Frisbee almost every time it was thrown—even when Mr. Connors put his special spin on it. He wasn't quite as good as Pete, but he certainly came close.

"You're some dog, Buster," Cricket's father laughed. "But I'm afraid you've worn me out."

"Me, too," said Cricket, trying to dodge the slobbery Frisbee that Buster kept shoving at her. How could that little old lady have kept up with him? she wondered. And where in the world was she now? She dropped down on the lawn where Buster, who'd finally given up on the Frisbee, was lying, panting in the cool grass. Leaning back, she rested her head against his side, just as she used to do with Pete. Maybe the lady would never show up, she thought. Maybe she and Buster could lie here forever.

Then, just as she'd closed her eyes and was imagining the two of them playing in a Frisbee tournament, the doorbell rang.

"I'll bet that's Buster's owner now," Mr. Connors said, getting up from his seat on the deck. "I sort of hate to see him leave, but I guess he has to."

"Maybe I can go to her house and play with him sometime," Cricket said as they headed inside, Buster at her heels. "I could take him to the park. He could certainly use the exercise. Maybe I could even dog-sit on weekends."

"That sounds like a good idea," said Mr. Connors. They reached the living room just as Cricket's mother, who'd been reading the Sunday paper, opened the front door.

Cricket expected to see the little gray-haired lady from the pet shop standing on the steps. Instead, she saw a short, bald-headed man. His jacket and slacks were wrinkled, as if he'd slept in them all night, and his eyes, behind his metal-rimmed glasses, were red and tired-looking.

"Is this the Connors's residence?" he asked. Cricket noticed that he was holding one of their flyers in his hand.

"Yes, it is," said her mother, noticing the flyer, too. "I'm afraid you're a day late, though. The dog wash was yesterday."

"Yes, I know. That's why I'm—" But before he could finish his sentence, Buster let out a woof and bounded across the room. He leaped up on the man, almost knocking off his glasses. "Stop that!" the man exclaimed. He caught hold of the doorjamb to keep from losing his balance. "That's enough, Buster. Down, I say, down!"

Cricket grabbed Buster by the collar and pulled him away. She didn't like the way the man had yelled at him. Buster was just trying to be friendly, after all. And he obviously knew the man. "Who are you?" she asked suspiciously. "Where's Buster's owner? He had to stay here all night. How could she have forgotten him like that?"

"Cricket," Mrs. Connors warned. A pained expression had come over the man's face.

"Please come in," said Cricket's father, stepping forward and holding out his hand. "I'm David Connors, and this is my wife, Karen, and my daughter, Cricket."

"Thank you," the man said, keeping an eye on Buster as he straightened his glasses. He shook Mr. Connors's hand. "I'm John Harris. Mary Harris, Buster's owner, is my mother."

"But where is she? Why didn't she come back for him?" Cricket demanded, hanging onto Buster's collar. The man might be that nice lady's son, but she still didn't like him.

"I . . . I'm afraid she had an accident," Mr. Harris replied. "She fell down yesterday afternoon and broke her hip. I've been with her at the hospital all night. She was in a lot of pain and it wasn't until this morning that she was able to tell me about Buster. It's funny," he said, with a wry smile. "But I was always afraid that dog would make Mom hurt herself one day. Yet it happened when he wasn't even around."

"Oh, dear. I'm so sorry, Mr. Harris," said Cricket's mother kindly. "Please sit down. Perhaps you'd like a cup of coffee."

"That's very kind of you, but no," Mr. Harris said, declining the coffee, but sitting on the edge of the sofa. "I can't stay long. I have to get back to the hospital. But my mother insisted I come here first and see about Buster. I hope he hasn't been too much trouble," he said, looking at Buster as if he couldn't imagine him *not* being trouble.

"No, not at all," replied Mr. Connors. He cast a quick glance at Cricket, who was having a hard time being polite, even though she couldn't help feeling sorry for someone whose mother was in the hospital. "Buster's got a lot of energy, but we've enjoyed having him. About your mother, though—will she be all right?"

"Oh, yes," said Mr. Harris, brightening. "She'll be operated on tomorrow. They can do wonders with hip replacements these days. Once she's out of the hospital she'll come to live with me and my wife in San Francisco. It'll be much better for her there. We've been trying to convince her to do it for years."

"But what about Buster?" Cricket blurted out, unable to keep silent any longer. "Do you have a yard? Is there a place for him to run?" She pulled the dog closer to her side. She'd probably never get to see him again if he moved to San Francisco. She certainly wouldn't be able to take him for walks in the park.

Mr. Harris looked at Cricket and Buster uncomfortably. "I'm afraid he won't be coming with us," he said. "We can't have a dog where we live, and he's really too much for an older person like my mother. Even she admits that. It's only because she has such a tender heart that she took him in."

"But . . . but where will he go?" asked Cricket.

"To the county animal shelter," the man replied bluntly. "I told Mom she should take him there when she first found him, but she wouldn't do it. And now look what's happened," he said, apparently forgetting that Buster had nothing to do with his mother's fall.

Cricket couldn't believe what she was hearing. This

man didn't care about Buster. He didn't even like him. He planned to take him to the shelter just to get him off his hands. They'd lock him away in one of those runs with blue tags, and then in two weeks . . . "But you can't do that!" she cried, throwing her arms around Buster. "They'll kill him!"

"Oh, I don't think they'll do that, Cricket," said Mr. Connors quickly. "Someone's sure to adopt a friendly young dog like Buster. He'll find a good home."

"But he already has a good home!" Cricket exclaimed.

Mr. Harris shook his head. "I'm afraid you don't understand," he said, as if Cricket were a two-year-old. "I said that my mother can't—"

"I mean *here*," Cricket interrupted. "He can stay here. Can't he, Mom? Dad?" She turned to her parents. "We can adopt him right now. He doesn't have to go to the animal shelter at all!"

"Why, Cricket . . ." Mrs. Connors looked surprised. "What about the puppies? I thought that—"

"I don't want a puppy!" Cricket cried. "I want Buster!" The moment she said it, she knew it was true. Just last week, she'd wanted one of Cindy's puppies more than anything else in the world. But now . . . well . . . now she loved Buster. There was no other way to describe it, no other way to explain. He was big and warm and friendly and smart—just like Pete had been. He was everything she'd ever wanted in a dog. She couldn't imagine having any dog but him.

"Could we keep him, Dad?" she asked. "Please? I promise I'll take him to obedience classes. I won't let him dig any more holes in the garden or chew on your tennis racket."

Mr. Connors's eyebrows shot up at that. He obviously hadn't known about the tennis racket.

"I'll help pay for his food," she rushed on. "And I won't let him bother the new baby, either. Remember, it's good for a child to be raised with a dog—a nice big dependable dog like Buster."

"Well, I have to admit I've gotten kind of attached to him myself," said Mr. Connors, not mentioning the tennis racket. He looked at his wife.

"Are you sure, Cricket?" Mrs. Connors asked. "It wouldn't be fair to take him and then change your mind."

"I'm absolutely sure," Cricket said. And she was. "Can I keep him, Mr. Harris?" she asked earnestly. "I'm sure your mother would agree. She could come see him anytime she wants. I could even bring him to visit you in San Francisco."

"Oh, I don't think that will be necessary," said Mr. Harris quickly. "But I'm sure that if he stayed here my mother would be very happy. I wasn't looking forward to telling her I had to bring him to the shelter." He stood up, looking as if a load had been lifted from his shoulders. "Well, this has certainly turned out differently than I'd expected," he said. "Let me leave you my number, just in case you change your minds."

"Don't worry," said Cricket. "We won't!"

Buster barked in agreement.

Mr. Harris insisted on paying the club's fee for washing Buster, even though Cricket assured him he didn't have to. "A deal's a deal," he said, smiling pleasantly for the first time since he'd arrived. "I'm in business myself and I always like to encourage enterprising young people. I think I may have some competition from you and your friends in years to come." He promised to bring his mother to visit as soon as she was able. And he was even nice—or at least, nicer—to Buster. "I've been a bit hard on him, I guess," he admitted, patting him gingerly on the head as he said good-bye. "I know he's a good-hearted dog with lots of love to give. I'm glad he's found someone young enough and strong enough to take it!"

What happened next didn't exactly surprise Cricket, though it might have if so many other surprising things hadn't already happened.

First, after Mr. Harris had left and Cricket and Buster had managed to calm down, Meg and Amy and Brittany arrived. Then everything about Buster had to be explained and re-explained, and the story of how Cricket had saved him had to be told and retold. Buster, who kept hearing his name mentioned, raced around giving everyone kisses. He repeated his bagel trick not once, but three times. It wasn't hard for the girls to understand how Cricket had fallen in love with him after that!

"We still have to choose someone to spend the

money, though," Meg reminded them. "Even if you're not planning on getting one of Cindy's puppies." She was already thinking of the airplane ticket for Jenny. Now if she was chosen, she wouldn't have to worry about hurting Cricket.

"That's right," agreed Amy, thinking of sports camp and Rollerblades and tennis rackets. "Let's count the money now and see how much we've got."

The cookie tin on the kitchen counter turned out to contain $115. When Brittany added the $25 she'd collected for the last load of dogs they'd driven home, and Cricket added two IOUs for $5 each, they found that they had $150 in all.

"Wow!" said Meg. "That's better than I ever imagined we'd do. We can donate fifty dollars to the animal shelter and still have one hundred dollars left for whoever's name is picked out of the hat. Do you have one, Cricket?" she asked. "A hat, I mean. I forgot to bring the straw one from the attic."

Cricket dashed to her room, rummaged around in the closet, and found the old top hat she'd used in a magic show at school. There weren't any rabbits in it waiting to be pulled out, but suddenly she noticed something else, sitting on her desk by the closet. Meg's bear! She still hadn't returned it. How could she have forgotten? Dropping the bear into the hat, she hurried back to the kitchen.

"Oh, Cricket, that's perfect," said Brittany, when she saw the hat.

Meg turned it over to put on her head and the little bear fell out. "My teddy bear!" she exclaimed, picking up the bear from the floor before Buster could grab it. "I've been looking all over for him. How did he get in here?"

"Sorry," Cricket said. "I put it in my pocket for luck last Saturday and forgot to give it back."

Meg clutched the bear happily. "That's okay," she said. "I'm just glad to have him back. But I'm going to have to apologize to poor Kevin. I was sure he must have taken it." She slipped the bear into her pocket, thinking that maybe Cricket was right. Maybe it did have luck-giving powers. It had worked for her, after all, though in a pretty roundabout way.

"All right now, everyone put in your name," directed Brittany, passing out slips of paper. Scarcely thinking about winning, Cricket wrote her name and dropped it into the hat. Brittany, who wasn't taking part in the contest this time, shook the hat and swirled the names around. Then, closing her eyes, she reached in and picked one. "And the winner is. . ." She unfolded the paper. Her eyes opened wide. "Cricket!" she announced, breaking out in a smile.

"Incredible!" exclaimed Amy. "Whenever you don't need something, that's when you get it! I'll bet I get chosen to come up with the next project, just because I don't have a clue what we should do."

And she was.

"Oh no," she groaned, tugging at her ponytails dramatically. "Well, don't expect me to think up a project too soon. We still have to recover from this one!"

Brittany counted $100 out of the cookie tin and handed it to Cricket. "Now that you're not getting a puppy, what will you spend it on?" she asked.

"On Buster!" Cricket replied without a moment's hesitation. "I'm going to sign us up for obedience classes, and I promised my parents I'd help pay for his food. I'll get him a name tag, too. Can't forget that." She stopped, as if she'd suddenly thought of something. "And I'm going to get something else, too," she added mysteriously. "Something for all of us."

"What?" Meg said. "Tell."

But Cricket wouldn't.

It wasn't until the following Saturday that the girls found out Cricket's secret. Cricket invited all of them over for brownies and chocolate chip cookies. Luckily, her mother was into chocolate now, not pickles and chilies! She planned to take the girls to visit the Sunny Hill Kennels afterward. "No reason not to come see the puppies, even though you're not getting one," said Mrs. Wilson when she called. "And bring Buster with you. I want to meet him!" First, though, Cricket had to give them her surprise. Next to each girl's plate on the dining room table, she placed a small, ribbon-wrapped box.

Amy was the first to open hers. "Oh, Cricket!" she exclaimed, lifting out a small silver-colored heart strung on a pink velvet ribbon. On the surface of the heart were engraved the words *Always Friends,* and beneath them, *Amy.*

"Where did you get these?" said Brittany, lifting her heart, with *Always Friends* and *Brittany* engraved on it, out of the box.

"They're wonderful," said Meg. "But there's something familiar about them. Haven't I seen one on— Buster!" she exclaimed. She pulled the big white dog over and showed the girls the tag on his collar. It was exactly the same, heart-shaped and silver. *Buster*, it said, followed by the Connors's address.

Cricket laughed. "You've found me out! I ordered them from the pet shop!" she said. "We can use them as key chains or wear them as necklaces. And every time we do, we'll be reminded of the most important thing—that we'll always, always be friends!"

Don't miss any of the great titles in the
ALWAYS FRIENDS CLUB series:

Meg and the Secret Scrapbook
0-8167-3578-6
$2.95 U.S./$3.95 CAN.

Cricket Goes to the Dogs
0-8167-3577-8
$2.95 U.S./$3.95 CAN.

Amy's Haunted House
0-8167-3576-X
$2.95 U.S./$3.95 CAN.

Beautiful Brittany
0-8167-3575-1
$2.95 U.S./$3.95 CAN.

Available wherever you buy books.